MAL D'AFRIQUE

AND STORIES FROM OTHER PLACES

BY JARDA CERVENKA

Minnesota Voices Project Number 66

NEW RIVERS PRESS 1995

New Rivers Press is a non-profit literary press dedicated to publishing the very best emerging writers in our region, nation, and world.

The publication of *Mal d'Afrique* has been made possible by generous grants from the Dayton Hudson Foundation on behalf of Dayton's and Target Stores, the Jerome Foundation, the Metropolitan Regional Arts Council (from an appropriation by the Minnesota Legislature), the North Dakota Council on the Arts, the South Dakota Arts Council, and the James R. Thorpe Foundation.

Additional support has been provided by the Bush Foundation, General Mills Foundation, Liberty State Bank, the McKnight Foundation, the Minnesota State Arts Board (through an appropriation by the Minnesota Legislature), the Star Tribune/Cowles Media Company, the Tennant Company Foundation, and the contributing members of New Rivers Press. New Rivers Press is a member agency of United Arts.

New Rivers Press books are distributed by The Talman Company, 131 Spring Street, Suite 201 E-N, New York, NY 10012 (1-800-537-8894).

Mal d'Afrique has been manufactured in the United States of America for New Rivers Press, 420 N. 5th Street/Suite 910, Minneapolis, MN 55401. First Edition.

Acknowledgments

After my first published story it was my son Vojta, Marilyn Gorlin, Ester Wattenberg, Sarah Kustritz, and Carol Anderson who gave me much needed support and urged me to write more.

I would like to thank my daughter Tereza who reviewed all stories in this book, and her critique was invaluable. I would also like to thank my editor John Mihelic. Bill Truesdale and Patricia Hampl also helped generously with detailed remarks. Special thanks to Burt Shapiro, Bob Vickers, and Jakub Tolar. And to Yuichi Seki (Yusuke Keida)—mentor and friend—a cup of sake!

To my wife Sasha, the most faithful supporter of my climbs, dives, and solo expeditions, my abiding affection.

Contents

THE HAPPY FUTURE OF DVORAK THE KULAK

I ASKED FOR MORE DUMPLINGS soaked in that heavenly sauce. The baked pork chops with red sauerkraut sprinkled with caraway seeds, moistened by a dash of cheap red wine, and dumplings sliced thin by a loop of sewing thread, were ambrosia to my hamburger-sated palate. Then, a half-liter of Taborsky beer, which flows like milk, the foam cap not white but tinted with gold, tasting almost sweet, with the smell of fresh South Bohemian bread! But it was time to go. She walked me to my rented Volkswagen. I kissed my aunt's cold forehead, slammed the door, and rolled down the window. Waving goodbye is a must, here, in Bohemia.

"Happy carburetion," she waved, and I started the engine. "For dinner we'll have plum dumplings." (Dumplings again. Great.) "I'll keep it hot for you."

Soon the last house of the town of Merry Betweenbridges disappeared, then only the steeple of the church trembled in my rear view mirror. It had been two decades since my last visit, but, unlike me, the countryside showed no signs of aging. Youthfully green meadows, golden fields of mustard plants, ponds mirroring the serious-looking spruce forest, winding paths between the velvet of barley which looked alive, shimmering in the afternoon sun. It was too short a ride to Pleasure, a village so insignificant it did not have a church, just a tiny chapel near the village pond—a pond so small that one could throw a stone over it with one's left hand.

On the railroad crossing the gates were down. I stopped next to an older lady waiting there with a wheelbarrow. She decorated her withered face with a smile and adjusted her man's sport coat of the prewar fashion. I nodded at her. Between the spruces on the right puffs of smoke appeared and the unmistakable choo-choo sound announced the approaching train, pulled by the real steam engine of a fairy tale vintage.

"Disneyland!" I cried in utter amazement.

"No, sir. It goes to Jarosov. To J-a-r-o-s-o-v," the wheelbarrow lady corrected me. The gates opened and she beat me over the rails by several yards.

A couple of mute dogs chased the car as I passed the tiny railroad station, slowing down on the forest road only wide enough for one-way traffic.

I found the house near the carp-breeding pond, the one with the lighthouse of a stunted, ragged willow which I still remembered. I recognized my great-uncle Dvořák's place with difficulty. The plum tree in the front yard had grown up tall and now shaded most of the front of the house. A new picket fence had been erected all around, and a handsome, ornate gate was covered with climbing roses still in their fall bloom. They were the kind of rose that blooms even after the first snowfall.

Old Dvořák "done good" with this place. It used to be just a shack, deserted by the last game warden forty years ago. They moved Dvořák there, the Party did, hoping to let him fade away, safely out of sight— to keep him out of everything that was happening in Pleasure. They punished him for what he was: "*kulak*," the owner of the biggest farm and horse stables and cow stalls, and the most fertile fields between the village and Blahuv pond.

Behind the windows in the ground floor, there was a collection of cacti, mostly gymnocalycia, some of which were blooming red. Near the doorway, an abstract metal sculpture (named, as I learned later, "The Mobile Flag-Honorer") moved one of its winged wheels slightly. I could feel the presence of Dvořák now, when the dissonant sounds of several clock-chimes, mixed with a few "cuckoos" of different rhythms, reminded me of a collection of clocks Dvořák had started, still in my time. It was two o'clock, very approximately.

Before I could knock on the door, Dvořák appeared in the doorway. I always believed that his face was built triangularly to accommodate his smile—he could grin from ear to ear, narrowing his eyes and usually stretching his arms, too. We hugged each other tightly in the old-fashioned way and walked into the house holding each other as in a certain move of the traditional village dance. It felt good to have an arm on his shoulder.

Dvořák did not hesitate; he opened the cabinet painted with flowers in nicely faded colors and brought out the bottle. "Well, how about some 'breath of the dead lover?'" he suggested. The smile did not leave his face.

I recognized the spirit to be Fermet Stock, the bitter and deadly herb-flavored distillate of long tradition. At first it tasted as bad as I vaguely remembered, but after a few shots and a few cigarettes, it became quite palatable. It used to be advertised as a medicine for many ailments, but in larger quantities it was well known to be able to split one's head right at the midline. The kitchen-living room where we sat down was cozy, warm, and with a definite personality, as they say. One wall was covered with clocks, many of them cuckoo clocks, some of the monstrous-looking cuckoos not completely retracted behind the tiny carved doors. Most of the clocks showed the correct time, and all those that did not work were set to show five minutes before twelve.

"To your health! That's important."

"To health, to the health." The shot glasses chimed in contact.

The wall opposite the cuckoos' wall was decorated by an antique cross with Jesus profusely bleeding red from many wounds, two plaques with deer antlers (one a twelve-pointer), and between them the plaster death mask of Dvořák's old friend, the teacher Kocanderie. I don't know how Dvořak got hold of that.

"To health! Let the health serve us well." Dvořák filled another shot glass.

"To the health," I agreed. "Uncle Dvořák, you did so nicely with this old house. So nicely." I felt the "breath of the dead lover" warming both my intestines and my disposition toward Dvořák. We talked about old times, about his two sons. We smiled at each other all the time, knowing that we had to warm up first for the talk about the big news. Not to rush it. The big news was too important. I was sure it would be mentioned, sort of offhandedly, casually at first, as if it were nothing special, and I looked forward to that moment. "Do you still play the bagpipe?" I asked, after downing the fourth drink.

"Oh ya, I do. An accordion, too. Got two of them, now." He went to the bedroom—I could see through the door the bed, with the bulge of a one-and-a-half-foot thick down comforter, bright blue with red stripes. He returned, already squeezing the accordion in the doorway, the music blasting as if for the village ball. Dvořák walked around the table, singing about the young girl who was unexpectedly visited by her lover, how she wore a translucent nightshirt and how she knew it and stood in front of the window deliberately, and how the visitor chased her to steal a kiss. Dvořák was singing with a smile and sometimes made a grimace of surprise and sometimes frowned in faked disapproval. It was a performance well-rehearsed, but it still moved me. He sat down to sing a couple of more songs, never looking at me; he looked out the window, or at the death mask of his friend, or at the half-finished bottle of Fermet Stock. Just between the songs, he looked into my eyes, nodding his head as if to say that these are good times, when two friends meet.

Then came the bagpipe. What music it was, what a sound! I could not take my eyes off the blackened carved head of a goat decorating one part of the instrument. It looked like the head of the devil, so pagan, so fitting the sweetly harsh Bohemian tunes which I had remembered from childhood. We toasted again. I don't remember to what we toasted.

"You like the music, Uncle Dvořák, don't you?"

"*Muzika?* It does me good too, my friend," he said, lighting a cigarette. "You know, when they took away my house and my farm and chased me to here, one day I could not take it any more and went to see what was happening over there, at my farm. I went the back way, sneaking from the forest along the railroad tracks. It looked so different than I had known it, just a few weeks earlier. And you know why?" Dvořák looked up at me. It seemed his eyes were teary, but it might have been the effect of the Fermet Stock. "It looked so strange because they cut down the cherries, my cherry trees. I will never know why they did such a thing."

He looked into his drink and turned his head from side to side, just once. He continued: "And when I came closer and looked at the cherry trees lying down there, I saw that they were blooming. After they cut them down, they started to bloom. They were covered with fresh white blossoms."

"I'll be damned," I mumbled.

"It hurt me, here," Dvořák continued, pointing at his chest. "It pained me so much I barely made it home then. I lay down, and it did not stop, the hurt. I could not eat for days, only lay in bed all the time, looking at the walls, looking at the bagpipe standing in the corner there." Dvořák pointed to the bedroom. "Then one day I crawled out and picked it up and squeezed the bag and started to play. And I played all night. By morning, I seemed to feel a little better."

Dvořák told me how he played all the next day, then slept a little and played half of that night and all the next day, always feeling better. After a few days of playing the bagpipe, his fingers swelled, but the pain in his chest faded away, until finally it was gone. "And so I was well again, got me a job fixing the road, and after work I was fixing up this house and straightening up my boys, after my wife died, God give her eternal glory. I have been playing accordion on weekends in the beer hall, for a little money, you know. And playing the bagpipe, too, just by the lake down here. But that one bagpipe I play for myself," he added.

"I wouldn't believe it if it were not you telling me, Uncle Dvořák," I said, to dispel the silence. "I mean, how you have healed yourself by the music." This time he rolled himself a cigarette. His fingers, thickened by road work, touched the cigarette paper gently, rolled it in one flick. He licked the glue on the edge, then smoothed it evenly, holding the finished cigarette between the stretched index finger and middle finger, with gusto and a sort of elegance. He looked up at me sideways. For seventy years old, I thought, he is quite a specimen.

"I don't know what it is, here," he said, pointing with the cigarette at the left side of his chest. "What is it, under here?" I took another sip and just gave him a smile.

"You see, I have this girlfriend; she lives in Little Ponds." Dvořák leaned back on his chair and drew on his cigarette, the negative pressure caving in his cheeks, and blew a stream of blue smoke toward the ceiling. The room filled with the pungency of burning hay. Yes, it was the infamous Taraz Bulba tobacco. "She is such a pretty woman; handsome body, too. She could breast-feed half of the village. And I like her so much, you see, that when I just think about her, it hurts me right here." He pointed to the left side of his chest with the cig-arette. "I wonder what it is, under here." He looked at me sideways, but again I only smiled at him and did not tell him what is there, since he knew it damn well. Yes, for being seventy he did quite okay, I thought.

∾

The room was getting dark, and both of us silently understood that it was time for the big news. I knew about it from my aunt already, but I came to see Dvořák to congratulate him and to hear it again, directly from the old "*kulak*." Just a few weeks ago, the village co-operative (still polluted by communists) had returned all the confiscated property to Dvořák—all the stables, pig stalls, storage buildings and barn, the house, the fields, including the carp pond and part of the pine forest around it. After thirty-five years, they returned it all, or at least all that has remained. When Dvořák told me about it now, he looked shy, almost guilty, to my surprise.

We went to see the farm. Dvořák was in a very good mood, and on the way he talked about politics. He walked vigorously and did not slow down a bit on the steep, uphill path past the creek, near the farm. His eloquence vanished when we were stumbling over the junk on the barn floor, over piles of ancient manure in the stables, or when he guided me carefully along the half-collapsed floors of the house—neglect and damage everywhere.

"What kind of people could have done this?" he asked himself often. Then he asked me the same question. "What kind of people? It used to be such a place."

He pointed at the vast hand-hewn spruce beams holding up the roof of the barn, at the gothic sandstone ceiling arches of the spacious pig stalls, at the granite thresholds in every doorway, at painted tiles, some missing, in the corridors of the house, at the brick and stone walls two feet thick, at the sculpture of the bread-baking oven, at a large bath of polished stone with green bronze fittings and copper plumbing, still in place but obviously not in use for those three decades of socialist cooperative ownership. One moment Dvořák looked at me, sadly; the next moment he seemed to straighten up. We had stopped talking.

The sun was setting down behind the silhouette of the village when we started back. Dvořák was still quiet; I did not want to disturb his thoughts. Some distance from the farm we stopped, lit cigarettes, and urinated, each on the opposite side of the path, as the evening enhanced the earthy fresh smell of the fields around us. In its descent to the horizon, the sun grew to the size of an enormous disk, giving a reddish tint to the barley fields around us.

I turned around. Dvořák was standing there, his back to me, surveying the farm—his farm—in the distance. Then he turned around with the widest smile his triangular face could accommodate. There he stood, the old "kulak," his fly still opened, rough pants soiled by earth, old brown cotton sweater hanging too large on him, stretching his arms—in the background, his farm, his fields, his future orchard, his future herd of cattle, his future. About ten to fifteen years, I estimated.

The back light glowing on his white hair was creating an unruly, radiant corona. Right next to the setting sun.

THE DROWNING IN STARYK SLOUGH

*Some memories seem strange, but that
is only because things often are remembered
as different from what they really were.*

LARS HAD SEVERAL TRUE FRIENDS because he was sincere. However, not many people knew that his real name was Ilja, Ilja Larson. Everybody called him Lars, even all the guys from our hockey team, LTC Praha. His father was not a Swede as his last name would suggest, but rather a Russian emigré. Old Larson was Russian only in the way he was perceived. In truth he *was* of Swedish blood—born to the son of Swedish immigrants to Russia in the time of Peter the Great.

LTC Praha, which stands for Lawn Tennis Club Praha, was, in fact, the hockey club where ice hockey started in Prague long before World War II. The game was introduced there by a Canadian, Johnny Buckna, who was basically a Czech, Jan Bukna, born in a small village near Nelahozeves.

My friend Lars had an uncle, who was not his real uncle, but the best friend of Lars's father, after whose death the friend moved in and became "uncle" to Lars's. And in a way, to me too, but only in secret, since I wouldn't take the liberty of being so familiar with him. Everybody knew him only by the name Borodichka, which means a little beard in Russian. He had been clean-shaven ever since anybody could remember, and it was understood that Borodichka was not his real name. The question of his surname and family name never came up. He himself was a Russian refugee, escaping not from Russia but from Kiev in the Ukraine.

Borodichka was built slender but of a military bearing which stooped forward a little in his later years. A slim nose of a good size seemed to precede him. His lips were rather thin but without strictness to them. His eyes I remember well: they were the color of an old man's eyes (pale early morning sky), decorated by hundreds of creases fanning out from their outer corners. And his eyes radiated kindness in a way that cannot be captured merely by describing that anatomy. They remained serious even when the rest of his face smiled, but I was never sure if they were serious or sad. When talking he would never rush. His hands lay calmly and his eyes looked into your eyes calmly as well. His ears were definitely outsized.

He always wore the same cardigan over sport shirts and a selection of carefully knotted woolen ties of patterns long forgotten. Conservative, restrained, with a smile—that is how I remember him.

His own room, next to the kitchen (intended for a servant, I believe) contained the neatly arranged essentials of a bachelor fond of books. Bookshelves entirely covered two walls to the ceiling. Next to the third wall was his bed with an old-fashioned brass frame, made up impeccably, as if ready for military inspection. His desk was by the window, and, as might be expected of the desk of a Russian, both a chess set and *samovar* were on it. His *samovar* was a towering brass contraption that looked so strange and complicated that I was certain it made tea the mysteriously proper Russian way. Only later I learned that he had not made tea in it for years.

I never asked about the history of this *samovar*, suspecting it to be a personal object, intimate to Borodichka's past. Anyway, questions were always asked by Borodichka, in perfect Czech of somewhat archaic purity, with an accent as pleasant as it was exotic. He was interested in us youths who were aware of the general disinterest of most adults. His long ears were ready to listen at all times. He took me seriously, talked to me seriously, asked all questions with genuine involvement showing in those concentrated eyes. About hockey, about school, and, without teasing, about girlfriends.

The little I knew about Borodichka's past was told by Lars, who did not know more than he revealed.

Borodichka was a graduate of the Czar's Military Academy, then an army engineer and officer in the elite Tereshchanskij Polk of Kiev, known for its fierce loyalty to the Czar. When the Bolshevik Revolution erupted in Russia and the Ukraine he fought the Red Army of the proletariat, was decorated, and later never talked about it. When his White Army was decimated, he managed to escape through China all the way to Prague, where he met Lars's father and became his best friend. He never married and never made a serious female acquaintance in Prague. That was all I knew about his past.

There was one bit of information more. Lars overheard his father once saying that when Borodichka drinks vodka he becomes sad instead of happy. It is so because he remembers his love of the Kiev that he lost.

ↄ

Lars and I made the B team of LTC, dated successfully many fair hockey fans, and entered Charles University. Borodichka was kept informed about our achievements and failures and, if asked, he advised us in his restrained way. After the first year of higher learning I managed to get on a group vacation trip to the Soviet Union—to Russia and the Ukraine. Borodichka was the first one to know, of course.

"We will spend three days in Kiev," I told him. "Your city, Borodichka!"

He listened intently to my itinerary till I finished. Then without a word he got up and disappeared into his room. Soon he returned, walking quickly, leaving the door open. On the table he carefully lay an old-fashioned photographic album bound in purple velvet with brass corners and with golden letters in Cyrillic on the cover.

"This is an album of photographs taken in the city of Kiev during the time of my residence."

So somber was his voice and so formal his diction it made me apprehensive. He raised his eyes from the album, attempted an apologetic smile, brushed his hair in place, and straightened his tie as if readying himself for important rhetoric. He turned the book for me to see better and opened it to the first page.

"The Byzantine temple, Sophia Sabor, is the crown jewel of Kiev's architecture. It has survived one thousand years." He paused. "Survived wars, invasions, fires. And the revolution, which destroyed everything, as you know."

When we finished with his album, I asked Borodichka to name the one single place in the Kiev of his youth which has been dearest to his heart. I said: the dearest to your heart. He hesitated with the answer, looking away, as if he did not hear me.

"There is a place on the Dnieper River," he said finally. "An old slough, on the left shore. It is called Staryk. 'Old man' in Russian, you know. Almost the same as in Czech. It is the most beautiful place I know."

I waited through a long silence. "I used to go there with my girl." He surprised me with the sudden intimacy.

Then briefly, with a formal smile, he wished me a good trip and safe return, as one wishes a departing traveler.

In the laser bright light of the Ukrainian fall, Sophia Sabor was a vision only vaguely resembling the sepia tinted black and white photographs on the first page of Borodichka's album of photographic memories. My eyes were hurting from the rays of early afternoon sun reflected off the golden onion topping the main steeple. Six smaller gold-plated onions seemed to accent its dominance. Most of the passersby lifted their eyes, some slowed down, some stopped as if paying respect to their own fairy tale castle, then hastened away. I was in a hurry too, looking for a bus station, so I decided to return another time.

This was the day I hoped to accomplish the most important task of the trip I had assigned myself: to photograph the Staryk Slough for Borodichka. I was going to find the slough and make a series of pictures, the best still photographs I would ever take. Daily, through the last couple of weeks, I had thought about it. I planned the lenses I would use, the exposures, composition, lighting. Some shots I wanted to take with slow shutter speed, letting the wind blur the treetops to a dreamy image. Some I wanted to make sharp against a towering cloud. I would lie down by the water and use the wide angle objective for a view such as would be seen by a frog. Some pictures would have a fallen tree for the foreground and the depth of field would vary. I would do a very careful job for my friend. That was my big project for the trip.

On Chreshchatik, the weathered Champs d'Elysée of Kiev, I boarded a bus going to the river, where I disembarked.

The River Dnieper—there it was! I repeated the name in a whisper. Wide as a lake, the vast surface still, sandy beaches and sand bars on both shores, right bank high, the opposite shore rising just a few feet and covered by trees in golden autumnal fashion. A barge with a red flag the size of a sail was pushing upstream, but no other traffic disturbed the flowing oily calmness.

In my pocket dictionary I found the word for a "ferryman": *perevozkaja.* The one I discovered nearby was an old man, looking like a gray boulder in his loose quilted pants and heavy army coat, dressed ready for a sudden blizzard, which, I guessed, would come in about two months. He took me into his wooden skiff with an outboard motor of ancient vintage, and I made it over the river with that pleasant excitement one feels crossing a body of unknown water.

Indeed, the old timer knew about Staryk. Not far downstream from here, he assured me, the first slough cutting in from the mainstream, right across from Pitchevskaja Lavra monastery on the other side. I found it easily.

The waters of Staryk became darker but more transparent as I proceeded along its sandy shore farther inland. The banks became gradually devoid of the debris left from the spring flood, the smell of decay decreased in intensity, and frogs called louder their claim for this pleasant stillwater. The aspens and willows, now in their most brilliant yellow, shared their gold with the ground. Everything shone brightly, smelled clean with the leaves and water and sun of fall. It is a beautiful place, Borodichka had said in Prague.

I photographed, changing exposures, depth of field, and composition. With some shots I waited for the breeze to subside so not a leaf would shiver; others I blurred intentionally. I finished the roll of film unsure as always about the results, put the equipment in my rucksack, and walked farther upstream. There, by a little bay, near an aspen sawyer with roots in the air, sat a fisherman with a long cane rod supported by a stick forked in a V at the end. Not the bobber on the water but a book in his hands held his attention.

He answered my greeting *"priviet"* with surprise on his face. Maybe seventy years old, I guessed by his face with high cheek bones, wide mouth, bulbous nose, and narrow eyes hiding under the bush of eyebrows. A Russian *mujik*'s face, I thought.

He closed the book, pushed his round wire glasses on to the tip of his Slavic proboscis, and gave me a long look, a welcoming look, I realized with some relief.

I asked him about the efficiency of fishing with a book in his hands.

"I am just giving a bath to the worm, young man," he said. "It is in no danger where it bathes now." He pointed to the bobber and put the book carefully on a stump next to him, indicating that we might converse.

"But there might be a fish passing by that will like your worm," I said.

"No, it is not possible," he smiled. "There are a few carp, *kasha*, in the middle of the slough, but they feed on the bottom. As friendly as kittens they are." He appeared to enjoy this subject. "It is true, the eel might pass by unannounced. Now in the fall it is the time for them to migrate, but they are becoming rare. Not like in the old times." He raised his hand in the gesture of futility.

Knowing the answer I asked "Have you been fishing here before?"

"For fifty years." He nodded. "For half a century. I know every centimeter of this place like I knew my *babushka*, God save her soul." The smile did not leave his face, which seemed to me younger now, almost handsome, for a *mujik*.

"You might ask, what will happen if I cast it right next to that fallen tree down there," he said. "I'll tell you that it will tempt the catfish, the *som*, which has been lounging there for years." He stretched his arms apart in the time-honored fisherman's gesture. "The biggest fish around, the *som*, real *molodiets!*"

"Over a meter?" I asked.

"Over a meter, and some. I pulled him out a few times, so we are friends by now. You see?"

"Isn't it good to eat, the som?"

"Would you eat a friend?"

I liked his laugh. It came from the depth of his bowels, like the sound of the bass bombardon playing staccato.

"Heaven forbid," he continued. "You look to me like a gentle-man, *kulturnyi chelovek, komilfo.* You wouldn't!"

Out of a well-worn German army backpack with a calfskin cover flap he pulled out an aluminum field flask. It had many scars and de-pressions, a long history. He unscrewed it and passed it to me. I sat down next to him and took a swig of it, cautiously. But it was Russ-ian vodka, powerful but smooth, went down like olive oil with no af-tertaste, and heated the entrails instantly in a miracle of physiology. I thanked the fisherman-reader and returned the flask for his turn.

"I was taking some photographs here for a friend of mine," I told him while he took a sip. He paid no attention.

"If I threw the worm to the bend over there," he pointed with the flask, "and if I pulled it in as one would pull a lure, I'd bring in a walleye, a *sudak.* Pure silver with a touch of gold on the gills. That is the fish to eat, the best you have ever tasted!" He looked at me as if expecting disapproval. "So good and pretty, it is a pity for a plain fisherman like me to kill a fish like that."

He continued: "But once a week I'll cast the bait—a ball made of bread is the best. I'll cast it right in the middle where the slough narrows. *Plotva* and *yaz* are always there scrounging around. Ay-a, how good for *ukha* soup!" He licked his lips in exaggeration. "Few potatoes in it, some veggies, any you can get will do. And you must use the heads with the eyes still in them—for the consis-tency—and cook it very, very slow. *Kievskaja ukha*—a rare delicacy, my friend."

I was getting hungry. The sun was diving behind the aspens, mak-ing them dark against the light, and the mirror of Staryk was broken by the black shadows of trees falling on it sharply. We shared the alu-minum flask and again I told him about having made some pho-tographs for an old friend of mine, a Czarist officer living in Prague, who used to come here in the old times. I hoped to talk about those old times on Staryk.

"Of those years I remember everything, molodiets," he said. "The trouble is I don't remember what happened yesterday, or an hour ago. That is the truth."

I stood up but still asked a question.

"Was it different here, then—the Staryk?"

"Everything about Kiev is different now, but Staryk is the same," he said. "That's why I come here."

"And how about the officers in the old times? Did they use to come here? Before the Bolsheviks, I mean. My friend told me he used to come here with his girlfriend."

"They would rarely come. Just one. Or two. They liked to walk down the Chreshchatik in their fancy uniforms. Oh ya."

"The Tereshchankskij Polk used to be stationed here in Kiev, I heard."

"Tereshchanskij—what a glory! But their officers, they were all killed by Bolsheviks, or escaped abroad, who knows where. Oh, were they a sight! They had the fanciest uniforms you have ever seen, ever."

"Pretty?" I asked.

"Pretty? All the girls in Kiev, and married ones too," he chuckled, "they all dreamt to have an officer from the Tereshchanskij Polk."

We had another sip of vodka.

"One of those ladies drowned herself right past this bend over there," he pointed. "In that spring after the Bolsheviks won their Revolution. I remember that well."

I sat down again and said: "What a sad thing, such an accident. I have been told there are pretty bad floods here in the spring."

"Oh no, my friend. No accident. She took her own life, she did. People said that her officer, her lover, did not return to her. Killed by Reds, or escaped abroad, that is for sure." He stared at the water. "Besides, I know she took her life herself because I found her and saw her face."

"It happened right here?" I asked.

"Right here. I was the unlucky one who found her here. And— this is what I want to tell you—when I pulled her hair off the face I was amazed. It had the color of ivory and it was so beautiful. Beautiful! I can still see her if I close my eyes."

We watched the bobber floating on the water in silence for a while as if in a tribute to the fisherman's memory.

"Beautiful, you said?" I did not understand the connection of beauty to suicide.

"I have never seen a more beautiful woman, dead or alive. Does it surprise you?" He lifted the flask and shook it. It was empty, its contents sharpening his memory now and enhancing my imagination.

"A woman who takes her life must first rid herself of the fear of death, you see?" He paused. "We all would be beautiful if we had no fear of dying. Even me." He laughed. "A woman is in her greatest beauty when she chooses death, frees herself of fear just before she takes her life. It must be like that."

He picked up his book with both hands and lifted it above his head as a sacred object of worship.

"It is all stored in books like this one. Everything amazing is said in books like this, my friend."

Then he reeled in the worm, removed its miniature pale carcass from the hook, and threw it in the water.

"My buddy *som* will find it with his whiskers. He has whiskers like a Czarist general—you should see him some time. *Do svidanija!*"

He said goodbye to the dead worm, packed his book and fishing gear, and we were on our way. Soon we reached the river where the reader-fisherman stopped. Across the stream of Dnieper, the Pitchevskaja Lavra monastery was flooded by the setting sun, its green steeples like theatre stage props against the darkening sky, looming high above the ageless stream.

"Dnieper—our soul, you know," he said, and we stood there watching her flow.

"She is our soul, that is the truth. Heavy, you know, deep soul, as is the river. Powerful in floods, peaceful and steady on sunny days. You cannot dam it, the soul or the river. And to explore her? Oh ya, ya."

I thought how lucky I was to meet a reader, and a fisherman to top it.

"But not very cheerful, you see," he went on. "Just like some great love—it isn't much fun and it could be a tragedy. Drowning. Not like the laughable loves, affairs that cheer your heart up and, some say, keep it healthy, even." He looked at me with a wide smile. "And that is why I go to Staryk. It is a love affair of this old fisher."

I wished we had some more vodka left. To drink to this old man's health.

"You are a foreigner, so when you go home to your friends, tell them you have met people whose soul is a river." He laughed with those sounds coming from deep within him and sounding the bass bombardon playing staccato. I thanked him and promised him I would tell my friends at home about the reader-fisherman I met, about Staryk, and the big soul-river.

He shook my hand with a squeeze as powerful as I expected from him, and we said nothing more and went separate ways.

Back in Prague I told Borodichka everything about my expedition to Staryk in the greatest detail. Everything, except the story about the drowning of the girl with the beautiful ivory face.

Then I gave him the photographs—eight by ten-inch black and white enlargements on semigloss Orwo paper.

He opened the envelope and pulled out the first one, the one with the fallen tree in the foreground and aspens by the bend of the slough. He held it in both hands. The leaves of the aspens started to shiver, then shook as if in the first blizzard of the Ukrainian winter.

I looked at his hands, then at his eyes, and I knew it was time to leave him alone.

MAL D'AFRIQUE

H<small>ARMATTAN, THE NORTHERN WIND</small> of the dry season, was blowing steadily, covering all of West Africa with fine red powder carried from the lands of *sahel*. It entered everywhere: into houses, inside cupboards, into pots, into ears, caking faces when mixed with sweat, making a ring of solid clay around one's collar. It swirled invisibly around the oven-like cabin of our van. Opening the windows did not help at all, but we did that anyway, hoping to relieve the heat.

The road cut through secondary forest, mostly bushes, palmettos, small twisted trees entangled with vines, in some places forming green walls, impenetrable without a *panga*. Firewood was scarce in this country, and all the hardwood had been burned a long time ago. Now, even dried ferns were used for cooking fuel.

I liked to travel this part of the road, passing the colorful markets, the children carrying water in pails on their heads, water splashing on their faces then being licked by pink tongues. Old men had a fishing pole or an antique hunting rifle, always with a *panga*-machetta in their hands. And there were sellers. A boy sold a small python, for roasting no doubt. A "man of the woods," with his bare-breasted woman, held a baby alligator. Strange pangolins were offered for sale, covered with fish-like scales, resembling the fossil stegosaurus. Or hunters sold duikers, the smallest antelopes, the size of a small dog. They dive into the bushes, hence their name.

Today, so far, a naturalist might have taken delight in seeing a six-foot black cobra crossing the road. We almost rolled the car over when my driver, Chukwu, swerved at full speed to hit it, and missed. I had to smoke two cigarettes, lighting the second one from the butt of the first, to calm myself. It was very hot, and after the first rain of the coming rainy season the humidity increased my misery.

After we crossed the small Ubue River, we passed by the freshly burned wreck of a minibus, still smoldering. As always, when passing the scene of an accident, I remembered meeting a white student on the campus of a West African university, the only European around. That happened on one of the first days of my stay here. Somehow he assumed that I must be a novice in West Africa, and he soon volunteered a series of instructions. The one I recalled now was about caution.

"You have to be really cautious, sir," he said. He was an eager fellow, with hollow cheeks and a yellowish complexion. I was sure he had gone through his malaria and amoebic dysentery already. "The number one rule is to slow down when the minibuses crash in front of you." Minibuses, like *matatus* in East Africa, are made to take about ten or fifteen passengers. To double the number is the custom in this country, and half of the passengers carry living hens and canisters with gasoline.

"When the minibuses crash," he continued, bodies lie all over the road, and if you don't slow down, I mean really slow down driving through, you are as good as dead yourself." There must have been some questioning expression on my face that compelled him to explain: "You know, if you go over them too fast, the bodies tend to wrap around the axle and wheel and all. And you'll go flying right—boom— into that iroko tree." I was not unhappy never to meet this nervous fellow again, but his bizarre instruction often came to my mind, driving the most dangerous roads in the world, African roads.

We were easily going eighty kilometers an hour on a bad surface, and still the driver enjoyed accelerating through the villages, where most of the business and socializing seemed to take place right on the road. Almost all of the minibuses we met played the old African roulette with us: the driver with the best nerves avoids a head-on collision at the very last second. After months of traveling these roads, I had to devise a strategy to keep my mental state sound and intact. It was not true stoicism or even fatalism: I called it "observatism." I had trained myself to ease back and simply observe myself driving, or sitting next to the driver, from a distance, from a safe distance— outside the car. And that was the state of mind I successfully put myself into, on our drive to the capital city, to the town with an international airport from which I hoped to journey home in an air-conditioned airplane, with a toilet, running water, and electric lights.

Would I ever again journey on this road in the opposite direction? Would I return? I knew the road so well, taking it to the hospital when sick, or to buy a can of Campbell's soup in town, or to attempt to use the telephone, or to have a couple of sloe gins in The Green Virgin, the infamous bar by the market. A few turns after the place we called Dead Man's Curve (there had been a dead man lying there for two days last month), we pulled up in a ditch for a break in our "flight" and to stretch. We got out right next to a simple roadside sacrificial place, with remnants of a chicken and dried blood on a clay pot with a few coins in it and a couple of cola nuts.

I used to be interested in these strange altars to ju-ju spirits, and I have always felt a little adventurous, seeing something unexplored, rarely talked about, and somewhat dark and secret. But by now I did not have a good feeling, being around it. It was no longer a cultural curiosity to me; there was nothing romantic about it anymore. It was too real. There were too many stories, too many newspaper reports. And most were confirmed by silence and resentment, understandable resentment, from anybody, even friends, that one would ask.

Not everybody was silent. The university students went on a strike with loud demonstrations for several days, when their colleague from engineering was found dead, his heart and head missing. The heart was thought to have been used for a sacrificial ritual, the head probably sold to a ju-ju priest. Around that time the newspapers reported the arrests of those who had sold human skulls at two for forty-two dollars each and one for thirty-five dollars—the cheaper one had been offered at a discount, as a remnant of an albino. All included the lower jaw. I also remembered now the embarrassed silence when, in the Aronzi village near my house, the meeting of neighbors was joined by a woman in a black mourning dress, the mother of a boy whose body parts were sacrificed near the river where the lowland begins, by a big tree.

"Prof, we should go. To make the city before dark." My reminiscing was interrupted by Chukwu, the driver. He did not feel comfortable around the sacrificial shrine either, walking around the van, faking inspection, kicking the tires.

"Why hurry, Chukwu?" I asked, knowing about his uneasiness and also knowing that there would be a curfew at night in the capital city, because of robberies and murders.

"No light on the streets, Prof. Many people walking when it gets cooler at evening."

Slowly the landscape changed from woods to fields, and more eucalyptus and euphorbias appeared along the road, not green but reddish or gray. Approaching the city, the road became pockmarked with more and more pot holes, its curbs eroded more deeply. With the decreasing distance to our destination, the spaces between wrecks in the ditches diminished until there was an almost continuous row of junked cars and vans and lorries, smashed into bizarre shapes, squashed to convoluted tangles of charred metal by both the losers and the winners at African roulette.

The number of people walking along and on the road increased too. I never tire of watching the lanky men in African tunics, worn dinner jackets, and an assortment of pants (from swimming trunks to bellbottoms) dragging sandals made of tires in their peculiar way—some picking their noses and chewing on a chew-stick at the same time. Often two men would stroll by holding hands, smiling and laughing in incomprehensible optimism. And the women—so perfectly straight, with colorful headdresses made of yards of cloth—carrying everything on their heads, from a postage stamp weighted by a stone to a tree trunk that two men could hardly have lifted. There went one, with a door perfectly balanced on her head and carried at a speedy pace. Her exquisitely sculptured face was decorated with a pleasing smile, to tell every passerby that her burden was balanced easily, of course. It never ceased to surprise me how most of the people were clean, in the midst of garbage and dust. Even the children, those ever-present benign vultures of medina and village, who screamed at me "*Bekee. Oibo anya acha! Anya acha!*" ("Blue eyes! Blue eyes!), and followed and followed me everywhere.

We had entered the city. "Chukwu, did we lose the way? Ebeki needje, wako?" I wanted to know. It had gotten dark with a speed usual for the near-equator, and we had turned off the main road to travel between the squalor of makeshift shelters of canvas, sticks, and flattened aluminum containers. The surface of the "road" now resembled the waves of a confused sea."*Odjo ato nage:* no worry, we go by river," the driver replied, and turned to me with an apologetic smile while letting the van go by itself for yards without smashing anything or anybody.

He was a pleasant man, easy to be with, and I already felt some sadness that I would leave him soon, having never had a chance to really understand the incredible abandon of his driving, his resistance to thirst, his constantly level mood, and so many other mysteries of his existence. He rarely tired visibly, could fall asleep in a second anywhere, any time of day, and never put headlights on at dusk until the complete, blackest darkness. His movements always seemed measured and sparse: only when he shifted up to fifth gear did he let his hand slip off the gear-stick, lifting it high before he brought it down on the steering wheel, so proud of his act of driving. The only thing we seemed to have in common was that we both sweated and, perhaps, smelled, equally as bad. And I liked that bond.

We had been passing a gathering of Hausa in long white robes and white caps, and scattered groups of Fulani women with their elaborate hairdos, dragging or carrying their children with angelic hamitic faces. "Chukwu, why are there so many people from the north here?"

"I pray that God would send the Saviour," answered Chukwu, turning his eyes up. The occasional surrealism of his answers was enjoyable but not easy to comprehend. His "acting" was easier on me than were his Kafka-like discourses. He "acted" his driver's tasks and his concern for pedestrians; he "acted" his rare anger and maybe even delight. I don't know if he ever distinguished his acting from reality— I have rarely been able to understand that.

Chukwu did not seem to act worried when our van was stopped by a gathering of agitated people, some screaming and running in different directions in front of us. The confusion increased every moment. We were surrounded. Chukwa stopped the van, rolled up the window, and motioned me to do the same—while invoking the names of several saints.

First a fist hit the windshield, then one hit the body of the van, then more and more, reverberating in a tremendous noise like a hundred drums. This was no ebullience, nor a prank. There was anger and frenzy on the dark faces behind the windows. I did not understand the reason for this, but very soon I saw the seriousness of the situation, feeling the fear spreading like catatonia through my legs, inside my belly. Chukwu's face became gray, a color I have known before—from the morgue. The van started to rock.

Then he—or it—appeared in front of the van. A tall figure was slowly approaching us, surrounded by a group of young men with sticks and clubs in their hands. At first sight the creature seemed enormous. Covered with a tunic of straw, he had a chain of bones around his neck, bells around his feet and wrists, a club in his hand, and his face was concealed under a wooden mask. He moved unhesitatingly toward us, spreading his legs wide with jerky movements, turning his head slowly from side to side, as praying mantises do. His guards kept the road opened in front of him, gesturing wildly, lashing with sticks at anybody in their way. When he approached the van, the beating on the windows stopped. The crowd separated, all watching the mask—and us.

An agitated crowd in Africa loses control easily, and often with disastrous results. I knew that great danger; Africans know it, too. Sweat was soaking my shirt. I tried to think. There must be an initiative from us; it was my turn for action now, even an action involving a risk. I rolled down the window and gestured briskly to the mask to come. With effort, I tried to look calm and, I hoped, to appear self-confident. After a pause (which seemed very long to me) the mask, with a few deliberate steps, approached, his hand with the club extended to the side.

Up close now I could see the crudely carved features of the mask, painted white, with black lips and black eyebrows, a black ridge for the nose and red circles around the hollows of the eye-holes. One foot from our open window, he stopped and remained motionless. A voice, muted by the mask but understandable, came out in the sudden silence of the crowd.

"Happy Easter, sir."

"*Dalo*," I said, thanking him. "*Kedu.*"

I had not seen his eyes behind the wooden face. It was too dark. Only cooking fires flickered along the road, their smoke mixing with the dust, the heat, the smell of urine and rotted fruit—the smell of a town at night, unmistakably West Africa, for which I felt affection at this moment.

We stumbled further into the city, over holes filled with water, where frogs gathered, roaring their mating sounds that resemble the grunting of pigs rather than the booming or croaking we know. I was very tired, holding onto the vision of a hotel room with a bath and a real bed. The hope of a cold beer seemed too good to be possible. We looked for anything resembling a hotel for another hour or so, sometimes retracing our way when a street was blacked by a pile of refuse. On one of these barricades, a dead body lay distorted in the beam of our headlights. In the next street we found a "hotel," a two-story structure owned by an older man in suspicious off-white underwear.

It was time to say goodbye to Chukwu. We shook hands, the Igbo way, softly, letting our limp fingers slip apart. We looked into each other's eyes, saying something meaningless. I felt some sadness but did not want to put it into words. It is not done here. Chukwu solved the parting by a sudden smile, a sad or tired grin. "*Kimesja*, Prof, *kachifo.*" Goodbye. Good night, without much cheer in his voice. He would travel through the whole dangerous night to get back home.

There seemed to be nobody around. Only the buzz of insects disturbed the silence. My room had air conditioning that worked. Full blast. When I collapsed naked on the bed, totally bushed, the electricity went off and with it the stream of cool air. In an instant, of course, sweat covered me and soon was soaking the pillow. After failing attempts to fall asleep, after turning the wet pillow over a few times to find a dry place, I gave up, put on shorts, and walked out. I soon discovered a veranda. There, around a table, two men were holding bottles of Star.

"Have a beer. Have one of these, friend." I poured it down my throat in one swallow: bitter, warm, but wonderful. The two Canadians were quite subdued. The young one, in his twenties, smoked a local brand of cigarette, one after another.

"You ask how it was, down there? I say it was not good—like hell.

No food, no water to drink, no soap, no shit. I was sick every god-damned day there, and I'm still sick," the young one said as he opened another bottle for his friend, using the inside of a lock on the door to the veranda as an opener.

The other man was much older, retirement age. His skin did not take the sun well; his face was covered with blotches, nose peeling, lips cracked. He still had lots of hair, reddish, with gray, now stuck together with sweat. He had a kind face, one with sleepy eyes and wrinkles everywhere, and when he smiled you saw only the upper teeth.

The two men were cartographers on their way home from several months of mapping the delta of the Niger River. The young man seemed eager to talk about the Niger. The delta was still unexplored, he said. Nobody dared go much farther downstream than Onitcha.

People live in the old ways there, he said, some still practicing slavery. The majority of people had never seen a white man nor traveled beyond their village. Some are hospitable; some look for strangers to be used for rituals or simply robbed and disposed of. And more. With more beer, more. Some of it I knew to be true; most of the rest of it I believed and found it interesting. My fatigue slowly went away. I brought from my room a bottle of palm wine.

The older man rarely talked, until the last bottle of their beer and the last drop of my palm wine (which I had bought from the village palm-tapper to bring home as a present). When I asked him why he was not happy—"Tomorrow an airplane, and home!"—it took him a while to answer. "Well, my pal died a week ago. You see? We were sitting under a big mango, near the village where we stayed. Black mamba hit him in the hand. Big snake." He nodded his head, looking away.

"We had worked together for fourteen years—for Shell, the first ten. There was nothing we could have done for him, nothing. He was gone in twenty minutes, André. It hurt him bad, too." He drained the last of the palm wine. "I'll have one of those—what the hell." He asked for a cigarette. "Just made the arrangements today with the airline to take him home to Quebec."

We did not talk for a while after he said the word "home." Then the older man grinned, and it was his first smile of the evening. He leaned back in his chair and took a long drag from his cigarette. "I'll tell you what going home means to me," the old man continued.

The mosquitoes were biting now. I feared the night-biting sons of bitches, having seen the many deadly diseases they transmit, but I forced myself to concentrate. I wanted to know everything about going home.

"Tomorrow evening, when I get to Quebec, my wife will be waiting for me at the airport with the station wagon, and we'll take off straight north. That's how we arranged it. We'll bypass the city; it will be late, not much traffic."

His face looked different now, a smile on it all the time he talked. "And you should see the country up there. We'll drive two hours through the forest: just spruce, tamarack, some white pine—real tall ones—and clumps of birches, white like the snow under them. And nothing and nobody there, just forests, and snow, and lakes, and it goes on for a thousand miles, all the way to the tree line by Hudson's Bay." His companion sat motionless, mouth agape, his cigarette burning forgotten in the ashtray.

"The path to our cabin from the road is not too long, and the neighbor plows the snow off it for us. You should see the piles of white stuff along the path. The last of it melts in May. Sometimes we already swim in the lake by then!" He looked much younger now. He paused, and his expression asked us if we could believe such a wonderful thing.

"It is still on the ground when the crocuses and the snowdrops have come and gone. In the cabin," he continued, "in the cabin I'll change, first thing—put on a thick Irish sweater and fur-lined moccasins. We'll make a fire in the fireplace—and woodstove, too. The fire will light up the place, and that looks real pretty, and smells great, too—the light on the knotty pine walls!"

This all sounded so strange now, like nothing less than paradise. The young man and me, we sat transfixed, trying to imagine the snow, the pines, while slapping mosquitoes, wiping off the sweat, in the humid heat of the night. "Then my girl will pull out something to warm me up, here," and he pointed at his belly covered with sweat. "I am sure there is an old bottle of Armagnac there. We'll warm it up a bit with a candle, and sip it by the fireplace.

"I tell you what I like to do before hitting the sack. I'll put on an old fur parka and light a pipe," he said, looking at his cigarette. "Then go out on the shore, just a few yards from the door, and stay there for a while. The lake under the moon, ice covered with fresh snow, so white you could see like in daylight; tracks of deer running along the shore, and tracks of otter sometimes. You know, the otter likes to run a few steps and then slide on her belly and run again and slide. It makes tracks like no other." He paused and continued: "There are spruces all around, with caps of snow on them, tall, reaching all the way to the stars—stars, like I have never, ever, seen anywhere."

He stopped talking for a long time, just smoking. "Ya, I like to stand there in the silence. So cold and so quiet—until the snow owl cries. So quiet."

I don't remember anything much after that. The next morning on the way to the airport, I didn't look around. My mind was far ahead of me, in the plane, somewhere above the predatory kites in low flight along the road, above the vultures soaring above the hospital. My mind was already in the plane that would take me home. Coming home I felt like coming from a war.

That year, in the fall, we bought a cabin on a sandy river not far from the Canadian border. In the winter I see the tracks of deer and coyotes dotting the frozen river, and the strange tracks of a playful otter sliding on her belly over the snow. At night, under the moon, it's as bright as in daylight. Then I walk to the river's shore and under the northern lights, sometimes, wait for the call of a snowy owl. My heart starts to ache a little, my mind fills with memories, of Africa. I dream of the Igbo girl singing her whole song with eyes turned down. I long to go to Africa again.

Africa.

I know my malady is incurable, its origin poorly understood. The French call it *Mal d'Afrique*.

POSSIBILITY OF HOPE

ONE WOULD NOT GUESS THAT 63 was a rarely privileged man, envied by most of the inmates working in the uranium mine of the Ministry of Correction and Justice. Slumped forward and gazing down, he was dragging his feet in the mud in front of the elevators to the mine. Those who did not know—new inmates, perhaps—would be surprised to see him enter the women's shaft elevator, where any access by a male inmate was forbidden under penalty of severe punishment. Women prisoners had been assigned to clean the old rubble and debris from the abandoned shaft. Since there was less and less high-grade uranium ore to be found, the old shaft was to be extended deeper, and new tunnels were to be dug out. The official reason for 63's descent to the mine was to take care of fungi. He was a specialist: the fungus-destroyer. He was thus allowed to work in the women's shaft.

The cage of the elevator fell rapidly into the darkness of the abyss, screeching and rattling at increasing speed. When the brakes were applied, 63 almost fell to his knees. He was not paying enough attention. He lifted the wire door of the cage and stumbled into the side tunnel. A few steps away, in the light of his headlamp, he saw the fungus. It grew from a wooden beam, in the same spot where he remembered destroying it, just a week ago.

This one was of a pale yellow hue, pitted, with dark spots near its attachment to the beam. These yellow mutants grew even faster than the red ones. It hung like a bag, at least two feet across. The sweated-out mucus had collected in droplets at the bottom of the growth.

Number 63 had been very careful with the yellow ones, but this time he worked without his usual concentration. He sprayed the fungus with a colorless fluid (of his invention), waited a few minutes, and switched on an ultraviolet lamp. Rapidly, the fungus started to change under the blue beam. Dissolving in some parts, crumbling and shrinking at the bottom, the growth seemed to tremble as it broke and fell in runny, jelly-like pieces onto the plastic sheet that 63 had spread underneath. The toughest part of the fungus, its sort of skeleton, had to be cut off the wooden beam, and the stalk had to be carefully scraped away from the wood.

Strange things, these mutant fungi. Number 63 had seen abandoned side-tunnels completely filled with them. And he would swear that some of them, the red and multi-colored ones, actually move when he approached close enough. He did not tell anybody about that, since inmates were horrified of them anyway. Some believed they caused the dreaded "cauliflowers."

❧

Today, before he left the barracks, 63 cleaned himself well. He wanted her to see him looking nice. With a piece of cloth wrapped around a matchstick, he cleaned his ears. He had hidden a tiny stick of oak-wood, chewed at one end—he brushed his teeth with it. Then he spit on the corner of the rag used as a towel and wiped his eyes.

He looked at his hands. The fingers had the same shape as the fingers of all inmates who had worked in the mine for more than a couple of years: the fingertips were enlarged and somewhat flattened, like those of a tree-frog, and the nails were thickened and creased and turned downwards like claws. The radiation does that; everybody knew. Number 63 had a piece of sandstone hidden behind a loose board near the head of his bunk. He had carved it nicely into an oblong shape, flat on one side and grainy, just right for filing the claws. He worked on his nails often, so today he just touched up the thumbs, where the nails were the thickest.

He did not like to look at his hands. Sometimes it made him so sad he even wanted to die. Since they had to live, however, he and the other men often managed to joke about the claws. They had times when they joked about everything, even about the fungi—but never about "cauliflowers."

❧

Still distracted, tripping frequently, 63 stumbled over the railway ties leading inside the tunnel. He had suspected something was wrong with her. Last time he was here looking for her, he was sure she hid from him. And none of her mates wanted to answer his questions. He could hear the voices of the women's crew, working behind the bend ahead. Bumping painfully into the wooden scaffold brought him back out of his thoughts. He leaned on the beam to rest, avoiding two new fungi starting to grow on its side. They were still colorless, as all the young ones were. He pulled out of his breast pocket—and lit—an inch-long butt of a cigarette he had saved from yesterday.

He remembered the first time he had seen the "cauliflower." It was growing from inside the lips of old Number 105, the "Professor," out of a corner of his mouth. It was of whitish color, the size of a pea, barely visible at first. Number 105 had been able to hide it for a week or so, pulling his lips over it in a way that gave him the expression of one trying to make a funny face.

But no one was amused, not even the new inmates. The rule was known to all, already by then: inmates with a growth, a "cauliflower," must be "recorded" immediately. "Recorded" was an official term for being taken away. Anybody "recorded" never returned, and their families never saw them again. How they were disposed of, and where, nobody knew, not even the guards. The cancerous growth resembling a cauliflower was discussed only in whispers. It was feared, more than one feared death in the mine.

The first woman appeared in the tunnel, dragging the water hose, measuring her steps slowly. She approached 63, giving him no sign of recognition. She was one of the oldest inmates, but it was impossible to judge her age by her face. She had developed the common features of all inmates, which made them look like sisters, like siblings of a doomed family, which they were. Almost like clones, they had all acquired large eyes peering out of deep hollows, and narrow lips retracted over the teeth and tightened as in a denial of speaking. Their complexion did not vary from an ashen grayness. The eyes were so prominent in their grimace that everybody knew the colors of the irises of their friends' eyes, and people were remembered by that—the most important color in their lives.

Now 63 saw the laboring women. He looked for her, for Lena.

She separated herself from the group disassembling rusty rails, and approached him slowly. Lena's eyes were the pale blue of a spring morning sky. Her number was 36. When 63 met her, several weeks before, he had amused himself by manipulating their numbers, finding that subtracting hers from his gave exactly her age—an age which, by now, nobody could guess.

Number 36 touched his arm, and he looked at her face, just for a few seconds. Rapidly he averted his eyes, wavered, and leaned on the wall to support himself so as not to sink to the ground. He recovered and motioned her to sit down on the fallen beam. They sat there, shoulders and arms touching. Other inmates passing by sped up their steps, looking away.

When the cold had permeated her, she trembled, and he helped her to stand, holding her hand briefly. It was cold and wet—still clawless; he knew now she would never have a chance to grow claws. Her eyes peered at him, expressionless and as big as the eyes of a night animal. She was so pale now that her face seemed to glow in the semidarkness of the tunnel. There was no visible sorrow about her lips. But from one of her nostrils, a creamy-colored "cauliflower" drooped, clearly visible today and to be even more obvious at tomorrow's compulsory inspection.

They both tried to distort their lips into a smile. And then they parted. He ascended the mine and walked very slowly to his barracks. Halfway, he looked up at the sky. He seemed to straighten up and increase his speed.

ꙮ

In the story "Immortality," Kundera ponders on shame: "Shame means that we resist what we desire and feel ashamed that we desire what we resist." Number 63 had succeeded in resisting his desire to cry, but felt ashamed of succeeding. Sometimes he became deadly tired of manipulating his own mind. Number 63 knew well that by now he was capable of achieving pleasurable feelings by refining the arts of survival. He had trained himself in it, just as a marathon runner trains, using mental discipline.

He had cultivated subtle skills for forgetting a disturbing event, dwelling on an achievement (however minor), categorizing pain into the realm of mere inconvenience, sometimes even elevating pain into a feeling of pleasure. He had managed, consciously, to put his mind into a frame of hope. Occasionally, he was aware, these efforts blurred the distinctions between reality and the imagination, but he assured himself that the means justified the end, which was simply survival. He did not know of Zen nor other religious philosophies of the East; his was an empirical experience. In that, he did not differ much from the simple sailor who survives weeks on a raft in the middle of an ocean. The only difference between them was that he had arrived at the state of required singlemindedness by a deliberate mental process. Like an acrobat, he performed his "satisfactions," and like an acrobat, he sometimes stumbled and failed. On this sad day it was too risky to fail, so he clutched the high trapeze of hope, with all his concentration.

Daniel Rosecky, number 63, in his fourth year of detention, sat on his bunk and took off his cap. From under the lining he pulled out a matchbox from which he removed a needle and some black thread, carefully rolled around a rectangular piece of cardboard. With even stitches he repaired a small tear in the sleeve of his cotton jacket. He put the cap back on his head again, to prevent any more loss of heat from his body—he must be careful about that. Then the boots went, and the square pieces of cloth used as socks were hung above the bunk to dry. He wrapped his feet in the blanket and sat with a straight back, leaning on the wall at the head of his bed, with his eyes closed.

Today, for fifteen minutes, he would imagine the town square with the inn, The Green Frog—his friends drinking beer, the barman Kadlecik explaining the winning strategy of their soccer team, waitress Klara in a miniskirt, play-acting revulsion at his friends' jokes. Then he would try to recall every detail of the stone fountain in the middle of the town square. When he could not visualize the face of the saint in the fountain, he finished dreaming. He rechecked the half-slice of bread in its hiding place under the loose wallboard, and walked to the window.

It was about time for the airplane. The plane, one of those from a great foreign airline, was on time, as usual. It appeared on the northwest and crept slowly across the vast blue screen towards its wonderful international destination. It left behind four white streaks, the possibility of hope, and a mirthless smile around the large eyes of Daniel Rosecky.

THE PICTURE OF FRAU GRAU

SERVICE BY THE PEOPLE, for the people! Closer to the masses! Acquaint yourself with the working class! Shockwork for Peace! Always with a positive attitude, forward to the Socialist Order!" Filip murmured, mocking the prescribed lingo of the Party while carefully tilting a shovelful of brown coal in the the glowing drum stove. Eight miserable months in this grim, gray hole of a town. But things are starting to look up now, he assured himself, sitting on his bed and looking around his very own new room.

It appeared pretty clean, with whitewashed walls, the bed okay, a sturdy old table and a chair carved in the Biedemeier non-style, and on the floor an imitation-Persian carpet. He had fought for this habitat for eight months, ever since he arrived in Broumov to serve in the local hospital—his first posting after medical school. The shy rays of the winter evening sun entered through the window, bringing up the faded colors of the carpet—real carpet, a luxury unknown to Filip until now. There were no luxuries in his old place.

He drank to his new apartment. He raised his glass (formerly a mustard jar—washed well to be sure) and watched with a smile the sun rays bending through the clear fluid of the 140 proof Slivovitz, that life-giving distillate from plums—a gratuity, sneaked to him by a patient. He felt his entrails getting warmer, and soon his spirit, too. It felt, now, as if he were inside a downy soft cocoon, with soundproof insulation added for complete comfort. He remembered having achieved such a feeling briefly, in his old room, only when he had climbed fully dressed under the thick comforter and made himself a cave there, just as he used to make, some twenty years ago, in his grandmother's bed.

His old room—one wouldn't call it an apartment—had not been

a very good place to spend the winter. There was no warmth from the stove, since there was no stove nor any other heating device. Entrance to that basement shelter was right off the street. The door could not be closed completely, so there was always a miniature snowdrift on the threshold inside, which changed size and shape according to the prevailing winds on the snow-covered street. Household insects had not survived there—not even a "rus" (for "Russian"), as that small species of cockroach was called, livened its icy corners. There had been no plumbing nor wash basin, so Filip used to wash himself in the hospital in a patient's bathroom, and he took a bath there twice a week on Tuesdays and Saturdays. His only consolation about the grim facts of his hygiene was that his patients did not bathe any more frequently than he did, and judging from the amazing intensity of their bodily odors, some at even greater intervals.

But all that was just a curious memory now. There was a regular bathroom in the hallway near his new room, with a gas water heater which actually heated water, and, after his bath, the coal stove in his room could be fired to a red glow, visible if the lights were switched off.

Filip felt himself to be a very lucky man: a nice place to stay, ownership of a motor scooter in nearly perfect condition, a new nylon jacket with a heavy brass zipper, and Austrian blue jeans. And he had a supply of good travel and explorer books.

Broumov was a sad town by any standard. About half of the houses were deserted, with broken windows and falling stucco, doors swinging with screeching sounds in the winter winds, weeds growing on the roofs, broken glass and rotted construction wood everywhere. It was a ghost city without the mystery of an old ghost town. It was a town ravaged by a war that actually never happened there. Just days after the big war was proclaimed to be over, all its inhabitants of German origin had been repatriated or expatriated from Broumov to Germany. The town had been plundered then, and not enough Czechs had yet volunteered to stay permanently—which attests to their native intelligence.

The young physician, Filip, had not selected Broumov of his own free will either, but had been assigned there, in part as punishment for his lack of political enthusiasm during his years at medical school.

This had been officially judged to be political indifference, regarded as an attitude just one step short of disloyalty to his socialist motherland. He was on the verge of being viewed as an enemy of the people—which would be a heinous crime always punishable by swift and often brutal action by the authorities.

"Authorities" functioned as authorities for the main purpose of taking care of lax fellows like Filip. A long time ago he had made a conscious decision to function as inconspicuously as possible, in order to avoid any contact with the authorities. And he well knew that in a small, grim outpost such as Broumov, far away from his friends and acquaintances with influence and "connections," he had to master the art of fading into the woodwork. That was his predicament in Broumov, and he had done quite well. So far.

"We're doing quite well, so far," Filip said out loud, looking with satisfaction around his new room. "Let's fix this place up real nice, old boy." This place would need some more furniture. No draperies on the window—let's get in all the light we can. But a small rug by the bed would be nice. And some posters or pictures on the wall.

∾

It was still dark when Filip entered the hospital. The hospital watchman, old Mrázek, greeted him with a soldier's salute. "How is it going, Doc?"

"Worse than shit, Mr. Mrázek," Filip answered, with his customary phrasing. "Any hassle over the night shift?"

"Thank God, it was quiet—like the woods. No drunken corpses, no battered motorcyclists." Filip sort of liked Mrázek.

"Are you going to be around this morning, Mr. Mrázek? I'd like to stop by and ask you something."

"Oh ya, my boy. My shift ends at noon today. Come for a smoke—just bring your own coffee."

Filip had to smile. He remembered what had happened a couple of weeks ago when the long-awaited electrocardiograph had finally arrived at the hospital. All the doctors had crowded around the machine trying to figure out the electrodes, levers, and gauges. The department chief had plugged the cable in and the gauges, trembling nervously, had indicated that no fuse was missing or blown out, yet. Filip, the most junior physician in the ward, was ordered to fetch some experimental human to try it on. "But not a patient, or we might get fucked," mumbled the chief. Filip disliked the chief because he was both crude and a party member.

Filip had tried to persuade some nurses, but none would volunteer—curiously, not even the ugliest of all, Olga, who always welcomed any task which would attract attention to her. But it took Filip only a couple of minutes to persuade the old watchman Mrázek to come and assume importance as the first subject to have a cardiogram on the new machine. They had attached the electrodes to Mrázek's white-haired chest, depressed under a respectable beer belly, and watched the abnormal curve of his EKG. Actually the peaks and valleys showed the classical configuration of a fresh and extensive heart attack, a coronary infarction. "Fuck this instrument. Let's do it again," proclaimed the chief, "and don't electrocute him." Mrázek looked worried.

They had repositioned the electrodes, adjusted a few knobs, and the EKG came out distinctly and clearly with the diagnosis of a heart attack. "Now Mrázek, what the hell is wrong with you, man? Either your alcoholic heart or this miserable machine is screwed up," the chief exclaimed. "You should be almost dead, Mrázek, according to this EKG. Has anything been wrong with you lately?"

"Oh no, Comrade Chief, I've been just fine," the watchman answered with uncertainty. "Only about a week ago, come to think of it, I thought I'd die. That's how it felt. But I did not skip a day of work, Comrade. I didn't miss one shift here. Only, riding the bike to work made me so miserable." Mrázek added, "Maybe I caught some bug. And my bike needs a new chain, too."

Then Filip, being the youngest in the ward, was made to volunteer to be examined by the machine, and the peaks and canyons of the EKG came out normal. That's how they discovered that the machine worked well and that the old watchman had just survived a massive heart attack, driving his old bike with a bad chain through it all.

Since then, Filip had liked Mrázek, excluding him from the category of ordinary men. (Filip did not trust ordinary men nowadays.) Just before noon, he stopped by the guard room, bringing his coffee cup. The old watchman poured himself a cup too, and asked Filip for a cigarette. "As they say, Doc, from the hand of a doctor even a cigarette is medicine."

"They say it about booze, Mr. Mrázek, not about cigarettes." Filip handed him a Papastratos, one of the new Greek imports with a filter. "This one should be for saving—at least a month from now," he added, feeling guilty.

"You know, Mr. Mrázek, I got this new apartment—one room actually," he continued. "It's small, but a real nice pad. But it needs some more furniture." Filip asked him if there would be some to be found somewhere in the hospital or in the cellar. Had there been something saved from the time before this mansion had been turned into a hospital? He only wanted to borrow it, he stressed.

Mrázek looked at the Greek cigarette, then looked up at Filip as if deep in thought. He assumed an air of importance, which worried Filip. "You should have seen the furniture, and carpets, and glassware, Doc, which they loaded into trucks in 1946—trucks coming and going all day. This was a beautiful mansion once, this hospital of ours." The watchman sipped his coffee. "And the owner, Herr Grau—he was a German and a millionaire, that's true. Strict man, stern character, that's true too, but I tell you—in confidence—he was a fair man. And a damn lucky one, to manage to get out with his wife just days after the war ended—just before they would have dragged him through the streets and all that."

"Did you know him personally?" Filip asked, wondering if Mrázek was avoiding the topic of getting the furniture for him.

"Everybody in Broumov knew him. And his wife Doreen, too. She was so young and beautiful—so beautiful, Doc." Mrázek lowered his voice and a grin appeared on his face. "I wonder sometimes how they are doing in Germany now. Wouldn't worry about him, though." He played with the Greek cigarette, put it unlit in his mouth and drew on it. Filip started to see his chances of getting some furniture today diminishing. Mrázek was in a talkative mood.

"You know, Doc, this cigarette . . ." He held it now like a pencil, between two fingers and his thumb. "This cigarette reminds me of my wife's brother, God bless his soul. He used to smoke these fancy Greeks." Filip sank down into the battered easy chair by the window of the guard room, sipping his coffee. He decided to be patient—and anyway, he liked to listen to the oldtimers. So he heard about Mrázek's brother-in-law, how he used to be proud to use only one match per day, lighting the first cigarette in the morning and then lighting all the others through the day, one from the smoldering butt of the previous one, chain-smoking eighty to one hundred— how he used to wake up a few times during the night, just to have a smoke, and how he used to throw up in the morning because of that. Also, how he had died recently.

"Right here, in the third ward, he died," Mrázek continued. "They said, the doctors did, he didn't get enough oxygen in his brain. Ambulance brought him unconscious up here. He never woke up. He lay here for three days, on his back, and never moved—except his right hand." Mrázek moved his hand in front of his mouth, as if taking imaginary puffs from a cigarette, in slow motion, in and out, and again. "Just like this, all three days and two nights."

Mrázek still moved his hand. Then it slowed down, and stopped. "Then his hand stopped moving, as the nurse, Martina—you know her—as she watched him. And his hand stayed lying on his mouth. That's when he stopped breathing. And left to be with his God, Comrade. He was gone."

They sat quietly for a while, and when Filip thought the pause had been long enough to honor the memory of the brother-in-law, he asked again about the furniture in the basement. Mrázek handed him a big old-fashioned key: "You know the door, Doc. The switch is right past the doorway. So take a look. Maybe you can find some junk there."

The storage area was wet with the musty smell of basements. Dust covered a pile of rusty bedsprings in one corner, next to a few chairs with reddish leather backs but with the seats removed. A couple of metal hospital bedside tables lay on their sides, drawers partly open, rust already eating them away. The only object Filip inspected was a good-sized office desk with a top that looked like well-worn hardwood. It stood next to the wall, with its drawers facing the wall. He tried to drag the desk from the wall, and after a few attempts only managed to move it about a foot. Another push moved the desk far enough away to reveal a painting leaning against the wall. It was frameless, the canvas stretched on a wooden rectangle. He brought it under the lightbulb hanging from the ceiling.

It was a portrait of a young woman on a dark background. Her light chestnut hair flowed down over the front of her left shoulder, her oval face illuminated evenly from the front. No part of her face was prominent. She had a small nose and good bones (as Filip's mother would describe high cheekbones). She had a tiny smile on her lips, which were pale, the color of her cheeks, not redder or darker. But her eyes were strange, and it took Filip some time to realize that they were of the same light chestnut hue as her hair.

He leaned the painting against the side of the desk and inspected it from a distance. The eyes followed him, wherever he moved. He knew this effect from old Renaissance portraits in the museum. It felt eerie, almost, giving the painting life. He moved his head to the left and to the right, and she continued looking at him, following him in the twilight of the basement. She was the most beautiful woman Filip had ever seen. She was even more beautiful than the movie star, Hana Vitová, even more beautiful than Ingrid Bergman, he thought.

And then he decided he must have this painting, and he'd do whatever it would take to get it. Sweat ran down from his armpits in anticipation of the problems he might have with smuggling it home. He briskly took off his white coat, wrapped the painting in it, locked the basement behind him, and passed the open door of Mrácek's guard room at a fast pace. "Nothing there, Mr. Mrázek—just an old picture. It is in bad shape," Filip shouted too loudly, "but at least it's something for the wall." He disappeared, registering the questioning look of the old watchman.

Light snow was falling when Filip hurried over the town square to his apartment. Since he was wearing only his shirt, passersby gave him strange looks, which forced him to increase his pace. This caused even more citizens to follow him with their eyes. He was relieved to be finally in his apartment, where he put the painting on the chair and sat opposite it on his bed, still breathing hard, his legs tired. In the better light now, her hair changed to an even lighter brown and her eyes, which were of the same light shade, looked at him again. He thought the eyes were happy, as if wondering about her new freedom from the basement. Only with difficulty did Filip force himself to return to the hospital where he hurried through his work. There, he could think only about returning to his room, and patients looked at him in the same strange way that Mrázek and the people in the town square had.

That evening, back at home, Filip sat on his bed again and watched her follow him as he moved from one side of the bed to the other.

These were the times of one television set per one hundred households. The country was ruled by the evil fists of the Big Party, with many little collaborators. This situation was reflected in the pathetic programs on television, on that one set per hundred households. And that situation made great readers of many citizens.

Filip was a reader. He read every night. He read about travels to exotic lands, about plants, insects, fishing, horses. He read about mountain climbing and hunting and sailing—and in between, poetry. He learned to use his books to generate dreams: daydreams, night dreams, and, best of all, evening dreams he directed for himself, lying on his bed before sleep overtook him and carried him into the realm of the night dream. He invited the painted woman into his evening dream the first night he brought her home.

Before he switched the light off, he had a long look at the painting, hanging now on the wall opposite his bed, so that when he closed his eyes, she would come alive easily. He dreamed, then. They sailed in a dugout canoe, hugging the coast of South America, rising and sinking on the long Pacific swells. The shores were steep, covered with jungle in many shades of green, interrupted with semilunar bays with narrow belts of black sand and occasional rocky precipices. On the rocks, they could see clusters of ferns, sprays of bromeliads and orchids. Collecting orchids was the goal of their expedition. They were excited by the thought of finding a species still undescribed, unknown to botany.

There was no place to land their canoe, no space for a night camp. Finally, in the late afternoon, they saw a thatched hut in the middle of a wide bay. When they approached the shelter, it became obvious that nobody was around. After easily landing on the outgoing tide, they inspected the surroundings of the hut and found the cooking place cold—no fire, not even the smoldering log which customarily is never allowed to go out in an Indian settlement.

It was a Cholo Indian hut, without walls, just a platform of split bamboo on stilts and a roof of palm thatch woven with the elaborate care and precision of people still living the old ways of the forest. A blowgun and paddle were attached under the roof and also gourds, with black and red paint, some colorful feathers, and the dried tail of an animal, covered not with fur but with bony scales. They concluded that the Indian family living here was off "visiting," and they hoped, with apprehension, that the Indians would not return soon. They prepared presents to be instantly at hand if the owners should suddenly appear.

They entered the forest. Filip could see her excitement, her wonder. Lianas thick as an arm drooped down, circling the immense trunks of capirona trees shining with wetness. Soon they, too, were wet—with perspiration. Still air and heat was proper for the jungle, so they felt only the exhilaration of adventure. They found orchids, and Filip climbed the renako tree to a great height, with ease, because of the helping tangles of lianas. He threw a cluster of orchids down to her: cymbidium with bizarre purple blossoms in thick clusters. She waved to him from deep below.

The sound of tumbling water led them to a waterfall. The water flowed like black lacquer from a cliff covered with dark green moss. Giant trees surrounded the waterfall like the walls of a cathedral, their canopy closing the sky above in gothic arches and making the sound of the water echo. They stood naked under the falling spray of droplets as an iridescent morpho butterfly looped from above and disappeared in the mist. They followed it until they could see the shore through the trees. There she found the rarest of Brassia orchids, in a cluster larger than had ever been seen before, with an enormous spray of blossoms of a faint lavender color, resembling rows of spiders in synchronized exercise, in exact position and distance from one another, swinging in the breeze which penetrated between the trees from the black sand beach.

Back in the Cholos' hut, they watched the rapid sunset. He told her stories about the forest—about the habits of dangerous conga ants which threaten both with jaws and venomous stingers, about the Cholos' practice of fishing with poisonous vines and their medicines. He told her about the sacred seven-colored snake, about the Indian carver blind from birth, and about the river dolphins with pink bellies and human breasts loved by lonely fishermen. And more. She listened mutely.

The darkness around them became penetrated by flights of miniature lanterns—large click-beetles with fluorescing spots on their thoraxes, shining brightly. Filip caught four of them in flight and held them up to her on his palm in order to irradiate her face. One shining beetle flew away, and another, and with each departure her eyes changed. When the last beetle had disappeared, her eyes vanished, too. Then there was just the blackness, and the sound of waves in the narcotic synchrony and music of the jungle.

∾

The next morning, walking to the hospital through the grayish slush of melting snow, Filip could not stop thinking about his dream. He was ordered to help hang a long red banner pledging his country to be forever faithful to the Soviet Union, and the disgust he felt really helped him to wake up. Mrázek did not mention the painting when Filip greeted him upon arrival, and later again when he left the hospital. Filip noticed that somehow it always started to snow when he was walking home.

His life had changed. He started looking forward to getting home as soon as he entered the hospital in the morning. He was thinking about her most of the day, planning to escort her, at night, into fantasies unattainable in reality. The next night he accompanied her to Nepal, to Mount Everest, the sacred Chomoloungma he knew so intimately from his books. He took her through the dangerous Icefall, where they admired the immense blue-ice seracs scattered in disarray as if the ice flow had been crushed by a giant's fist. They climbed the Western Cwm, ascended the steep Lhotse Wall, and after two camps, settled in a snow cave under the South Col. (He loved these names.)

And as she listened silently, as always, he told her about the history of the mountain, starting with Mallory and ending with her. They would not reach the summit in this dream. In the white silence of the snow cave, lying in sleeping bags, they could not breathe well because of the thin atmosphere. At this extreme altitude so close to the star-filled heavens it was impossible to think, to remember what had happened even recently, and they could not force themselves to anticipate tomorrow. Thus they were aware only of the present and only of each other, in the silence of their cave, falling asleep.

∾

Finally, spring came to Broumov: ducks flying over the sky above the town square and snow melting from the streets, raising the power of the creek near the hospital to that of a muddy torrent. The first rains cleansed the pavement and forced buds on the linden trees. And Filip became more of a dreamer. It could be seen in his eyes and even in his way of walking.

On this Monday morning, after the first cup of Turkish coffee, his last dream lingered in his mind. It had taken place in the lagoon behind a coral reef of a South Pacific atoll: all visions tinted blue, feelings of soothing warmth, sensations of wingless flight, weightless suspension. They floated, holding hands, above the heads of brain coral and forests of red gorgonias, between schools of colorful tangs and mullets and rainbow-colored parrotfish. There, a spotted moray eel faked an attack, and the log-like barracuda watched them without motion. The great manta ray, like a mutant bat, passed by undisturbed in its majesty, and a loggerhead turtle swished underneath, disappearing in the blue distance. They floated without effort, carried by the tidal stream along the changing display of miracles of a world silent and fantastic. They communicated with each other just by touch.

Monday was Filip's day off. From the window he could see people in the square, walking without hats, in light coats, and it seemed to him that not only people but the square, the fountain in the middle and the sky, too—all looked different. It felt to him like waking up from a very long night. All of a sudden he felt anxiousness. He did not want to dream away the real spring. He was sure of that—when watching wild geese flying over in a straight line that changed into an arrow. Their honking sounded like dogs barking in the sky. This morning he would go to the woods behind the hospital. He felt the need to escape the town, the medicine ward, even her eyes that followed him from the painting wherever he moved around his room. He was surprised by this new feeling.

He trod up the tall hill, inhaling the cold air smelling of wet snow and of pine resin, the silence hampered only by shrieks of blue jays from the conifers lining the loggers' path. From the top of the hill he looked down at the town, its ugliness decorated now with patches of new green and rain-washed red roofs. He pulled up the collar of his parka and descended into the trees off the path, touching their bark, making a snowball and throwing it high. When he surprised a rusty squirrel who squeaked in panic, he laughed loudly.

While he approached his apartment house, the sun broke through the heaviness of the sky, and he started to believe that spring was possible in this town. In his mailbox he found a letter from the Department of the Referee of Cadres of the city government, asking him to present himself tomorrow at a determined hour. That evening, he could not eat, moving restlessly around his room disturbed by this very serious matter. The most powerful member of the Party, Comrade Puta, was the head and the single employee of the Department of the Referee of Cadres. He was feared by Party members and non-members alike, since, in a small town like Broumov, he was virtually omnipotent while at the same time the least visible of all the gray and red potentates. Filip knew, of course, that nobody was called before this creature just for a chat.

That night she did not enter Filip's dream for the first time since he had brought the painting home. Maybe that was because he did not want her to join him in a dream full of strange fears and bizarre images. He slept fitfully, for only a few hours.

On March 15, 1960, Filip entered the office of the Referee of Cadres, Comrade Puta, paying careful attention to the movements of his limbs, his posture and facial expression. He managed to enter walking neither too slowly nor too quickly. His arms did not dangle carelessly, and although he did not smile he did not look unfriendly either. He managed not to look scared—he thought. Three walls of the room were lined up to the ceiling with metal shelves filled with folders containing the lives of all the town's citizens. One of the thousands of files lay opened on Puta's simple desk.

"Sit down, Comrade Doctor. Have a seat!" Puta's high voice was full of the kind tones one uses to talk with a child. "And by the way, happy birthday to you." Filip sank onto the hard chair in front of the desk, looking with wonder and apprehension at Puta. From the front view he saw the face of a weasel and from the side it was a bird, the profile of a strange bird. Nothing in that face moved when it talked, only the orifice of the small mouth opened and closed slightly. Prickly eyes, spaced closely together, watched Filip, suggesting no particular emotion.

"I almost forgot," said Filip, to interrupt the silence. He would not use the compulsory term, "comrade." He had never used it yet, and that had cost him, too. His posting to Broumov was, in part, the result of this little principle. But Filip did not consider his refusal to use the term "comrade" when addressing Party members as an act of defiance or heroism or a sign of a strong character. His acquaintances called it childish behavior. It made him feel fine, just the same. In fact, for him it was just a matter of convenience.

"And how do you like your work in the hospital, Comrade?"

"I like it," he said. "I find it interesting. . . . We have lots of interesting cases there. Plenty of work," Filip mumbled.

After a pause—uncomfortable for Filip and apparently enjoyable for Puta—the Referee continued, still using a friendly tone. "You see, Comrade Doctor, we were wondering." He paused. "We were wondering if you, by chance, might have some friends or maybe relatives living abroad." He took his narrowly spaced eyes off Filip and looked at the wall of files of the Cadre's Profiles, as in contemplation. "Not in England or France or Scandinavia, mind you. Not there. Those are interesting countries; they have beautiful cities there, I know . . ." He turned to Filip again and raised his voice: ". . . but in Germany. West Germany!"

There had been a confusion somewhere. Filip did not have any relatives in West Germany. Regaining his confidence, he said so: ". . . and no friends, nobody. All my relatives, actually, live in Prague. Well, not all are living directly in Prague; I have one relative . . ."

Puta's face changed suddenly. He narrowed his eyes, pulled the corners of his mouth down and jerked his hand in an impatient gesture to quiet Filip. He leaned forward, pointing with his beak-like nose, so that his chin receded even more. "In Germany, in *West* Germany. You have acquaintances, there. You know people there," he almost whispered. "Who are they? When were you contacted for the first time?" He roared now: "Who is he?" and leaned back.

Filip felt sweat on his forehead. He tried to compose himself but was not able to say anything. He tried to remember meeting some tourist in a bar in Prague, or any other place. No, he was almost sure he had never talked to anybody from West Germany, not in the last few years. And certainly not here in Broumov.

"I want you to tell me now, and clearly, who it was, when and with whom you made the deal, and where. None of us wants to waste time," Puta continued in a quiet voice again. "And I can advise you, I can assure you—it will be the best decision you can make, to tell me all—and now."

Filip calmly repeated his denial. He did not know anybody from West Germany and had made no deal. He said there must be some misunderstanding. He must have been confused with somebody else. He just works, nothing else. He does not have any foreign friends, not even many local friends in Broumov. Finally, he dared to ask, "What is this all about?"

"Comrade, you have made contact with West German agents recently. You are in serious trouble." Puta added, leaning back, "I am going to give you one last chance, one last chance to square this thing." He raised his finger: "One last chance."

Filip sweated. He felt pain in his temples, and fear tightened his stomach. Agents! This is shit, very grim stuff. He knew that this was no time for the cool, or even arrogant, composure he looked forward to enjoying just seconds ago—being innocent, having a clear conscience. Should he beg or perform some act of submission? But what would he beg for? And submissive behavior—he did not know how, actually.

While his headache increased, the grip of fear all of a sudden released his stomach and he felt a surge of adrenaline in his veins. He started to feel good, almost exhilaratingly good. He was overcome with wonderful anger. The weasel-bird face of Puta became somehow smaller in size. It looked pitiful, he thought. Filip had to suppress the temptation to smile. He stood up and made two deliberate steps to approach Puta's desk, and leaned forward.

"This is a serious accusation. And I refuse to listen to this, Puta." He was amazed to hear himself address Comrade Referee of Cadres Puta without "Comrade," even without "Mister." "You tell me, right now, what this is about? I have never contacted anyone. I have never dealt with any foreign nationals. I am losing time here, wasting the time of my patients." It flashed through this mind that he might have gone too far, but watching the change in Puta's features encouraged him.

The peculiar face of Puta expressed surprise, not offense nor aggression. "Please sit down, Doctor." Please, he said. But Filip did not give up the advantage of looming above the Referee. "I understand. I understand now." Puta waved his hand in a calming-down motion. "You see, we just did not know about the painting. We didn't comprehend why you would take it. Why you would take the picture of Doreen Grau home."

"What Doreen Grau?" Filip sat down. Hell, does he mean the painting of her? But he still did not comprehend.

"She is the wife of the capitalist Grau," Puta said. "You've heard about Grau, the German who owned everything here in Broumov, before we chased him back." He corrected himself: "Before he escaped to West Germany with her." Puta looked at his wall of files. His voice did not sound apologetic, but the tone of threat was gone.

"Return the picture, Comrade," he continued. "Do it tomorrow. Do it soon." He waved his hand dismissively. "It's just trouble, nothing less. Frame yourself a nice photograph or poster." He smiled for the first time, and Filip thought it was not a bad smile for such a face.

"But I still don't understand," Filip said. They both stood up.

"I see." Puta faked surprise. "Well, Comrade, we in the Party Directorate, we just thought that the capitalist Grau had contacted you, that he sent somebody, an agent, to get him the painting of his wife. You see?"

"To get the painting I borrowed?" Filip suddenly understood the situation.

"Why would anybody . . . for what other reason would you take such a picture home?" continued Puta. "The painting of some woman—in your apartment—you see? The picture of a complete stranger to you." He looked almost friendly now. "Honor to your work, Comrade." He wished Filip goodbye all of a sudden. "Honor to your work."

～

Filip sat on his bed and lit a cigarette. He still had some of the 140 proof slivovitz left. This was a good time for a shot or two. She looked at him from the wall, silent as ever. Her eyes did not hold any mysteries now.

Her name is Doreen. She is the wife of a German, of Herr Grau. She must be old now. She travels around the world with her rich husband. She might have kids his age, even—Filip felt hollow inside. The second shot of slivovitz did not change his feelings. There is no reason to wait until tomorrow, he thought. He wrapped the painting in a raincoat and adjusted the sleeves so they would not flap around.

At the hospital, Mrázek was still in his guard room. He was smoking again. They did not even exchange greetings, and the watchman took the painting without looking at it and without looking at Filip.

On the way home Filip sat on the bench in the town square near the sandstone fountain from which the statue of a saint had been removed. It was the first warm evening of the year. There was almost nobody around, just an occasional truck rattling by. He felt good now—relieved. He felt as if his whole being was becoming part of the spring. Maybe he would go tonight to a bar with some of the guys from hospital. Yes, that's what he would do. He stretched out on the bench, raising and spreading his arms apart above his head and looking up at the spring evening sky.

The sky, a dark blue ocean, was like the sea he knew from his books. The narrow rows of clouds reminded him of waves, of white-capped rollers coming to the shore. The ocean stretched over the roofs of the grim houses, farther away, far over the western border, thousands of miles. He saw himself in a sailing sloop under a great spinnaker, moving out of port, for a long, single-handed sail over the Atlantic. He carefully tied down the stored anchor, rolled down the mainsail a couple of feet, and on the starboard tack fastened the self-steering wane. He checked the compass again and looked back at the land, that diminished into a dark blemish on the clean line of the horizon.

SONG OF THE GENE

IT WAS ONE OF THE WARM and bright spring mornings: buds already opened in an unnatural green, premature daisies in the park—even a few subversive dandelions dotting the fresh lawns. The spring scent of hope was everywhere where the remnants of nature had survived the city. When Mike entered the room of the psychiatry ward, he felt an abandoning of spring outside, with all his senses. The white-washed walls reaching to the high white ceiling, four white beds, three of them carefully made up—everything was sterile, clean, with the aseptic odor of the hospital reminding him of his torturous child-hood tonsillectomy.

She was sitting on the bed smiling at him, the smile he had known fifteen years ago, at least. To see it, to see her here, did not do him much good, tightening him all up inside, as before a race or an exam. "Mike, how did you find me? Mikee!" He kissed her, re-membered the smell of her hair, put his hand on her hands—they seemed cold—and sat on the bed facing her, still holding her hands.

"You look good, Naomi. Real good."

"You haven't changed, Mike. You really haven't changed a bit. How happy I am to see you."

"Well, I was just passing through town, visiting my sister—you remember her? So I called your lab, and they told me I'd find you here. Of all places. But that's all they told me, Naomi." He paused, seeing her smile—still lingering about her eyes—becoming smaller. "That . . . surprised me, you know. Anyway, it's not so bad here, is it? Like—could you go out if you want? Any time you want, I mean?"

He let her hand go. It was not very easy to talk. He had always felt that she knew what he was thinking, somehow. She had always been "different"—as they used to say: best of the class in science, great in math, and what a piano player. Good at almost everything, she had trouble finding friends—or keeping them—being the best in high school. Less trouble in college and, he knew, no trouble having friends in her Ph.D. program. Right after her doctoral degree she was hired as director of the genetics laboratory. She married the first year she was there, and soon she had a kid, a boy. Mike could not remember his name now, but there had been some problem with him, with his health.

He looked at her hands. They had changed. Not like her face, which was even more attractive than he remembered. Maybe it was the trace of pain around her mouth now, together with the narrowing of her eyes, in delight at seeing him, which made her so strangely beautiful. But her hands were skinny, with a few bluish veins in winding patterns, the nails pale.

"Mike, I am so glad you came. I have much to tell you, if I can."

Mike asked about friends from school and about work. They talked about trivial things for a while, thinking how to look relaxed and at ease, until they came to a long pause.

"An extraordinary thing happened to me, Mike. I just hope I can explain it to you. How strange it all was." She looked at him with urgency. "But you have to bear with me. I have to start from the beginning." He thought it would be better to just go out, to eat and have a drink together, or maybe just to look at each other, quietly, for a while.

"You know I work in genetics, molecular genetics. Remember? I got the degree in gene splicing, recombinant DNA methods and that sort of thing. I got involved in the theoretical work—I really liked that." He thought it would be nice to take her out of here, at least for a while, and sit outside on the grass, maybe, and hold her hand again. He was not sure about holding her hand.

"Just a couple of years ago I came across this paper," she continued, with intensity in her voice. "It was written by a geneticist in California, Susumu Ohno, a very unusual fellow. He has been involved in so many things in genetics. Everything he did was well ahead of his time. Visionary stuff, some of it, and always appreciated only years after he published it. Anyway, he came up with this remarkable idea. He took a piece of DNA molecule, a piece of a gene, which had been sequenced."

Her eyes were questioning. There was something feverish about her, Mike noticed. It was disturbing.

"I know you are not a technical man, Mike, but this is not complicated in principle. Just give it a try, make an attempt to understand. You know that all DNA is put together from only four building blocks, bases—we write them as A, G, T, and C. And they are connected in various sequences. Like, for instance, ATCTCGCTTT, and so on. Do you follow me, Mike?" He nodded.

She told him how Ohno had observed repetitions of the groups of bases, and groups of their sequences in the genes, how he had decided that the repetitions were not promiscuous—yes, promiscuous, she said—but resembled a baroque musical composition. They recurred just as if governed by the principles of music. "Could you see that, Mike? Could you see the geniality of the thought?"

She told him how Ohno had assigned one space and the line above it in the treble clef staff to each of the four bases, A, G, T, and C, and how he had discovered that the treble clef in scores of musical compositions and in DNA compositions became interchangeable, how the genes could be written as music. Then he had assigned the DNA bases to Bach's "Prelude Number One"—and it looked just like the composition of a gene. And then, in reverse, he had assigned musical notes to the slime mold's gene sequence—slime mold, Mike!—and it sounded like a melody, with repetitions as in all true melodies. And more. He showed that a Chopin nocturne resembled the sequence for an RNA-polymerase, and that human PGK-coding sequence, when played on a violin: "It filled the listener with haunting melancholy"—as he wrote in his paper.

It was getting darker in the room. It started to rain outside, and Mike felt the pressure of an impending headache. But he did not move from his place on the bed.

He tried to imagine her sitting in front of him in a silk nightgown, not in this heavy flannel one. His mind made an excursion to the past, to their dates in the borrowed apartment uptown. He liked to imagine her lying next to him, to see her walking in her naked tenderness across the room. But even more he savored the memory of their cooking together or fixing the chair they broke.

He remembered asking her for a date the first time. It took him a lot of courage to risk it. He hoped then that she would help him, maybe with a little small talk. But she did not say a word, just listened to his attempts to be cool. He told her that he was afraid to ask her out because he was too short for her. He confessed, finally, that he thought she might laugh at him. She still remained silent, with a serious look, surprised perhaps. He chanced it with what he thought was a joke: "would you go out with me, the short guy? But not in high heels, Naomi?" He remembered it as if it had happened a couple of days ago.

"I'll come barefoot for you, Mike." Then she smiled at him for the first time, but she was serious, really serious. That was a long time ago. She was serious in liking him and later in loving him.

Naomi stopped talking for a while, as if knowing about the lapse in his concentration. "It is raining outside." She reached out and touched his hand. "*Yaruza-no ame*; the rain that prevents the guest from leaving, the geishas say in Japan, you know." Mike was looking away, at the window. Somehow he could not escape the memory so fast.

"I am some geisha! But this isn't any geisha house, either. Sorry, Mike, you had to meet me like this. But don't leave yet, please."

"I'll stay. I'll stay for a while," Mike said, "but I was wondering why they would put bars on all the windows, like in prison, or in the middle ages. That's what I don't like about this place." Mike was grateful for the interruption, for the change of topic. He had just started to have difficulty in following the genes and bases, DNA, and music, and all.

"Well, it's an older building," she said, "and I don't mind, really. They treat me all right here. Actually, the other day I woke up and the crystals of the morning frost on the bars shone all over the windows like brilliants, as if you had sprayed diamonds on them. It was really beautiful."

Now she looked less intense, almost happy. "I remember hearing an ex-prisoner, once, a prisoner of a Gulag somewhere in Siberia. He described how pretty the barbed wire was around their prison camp when it was covered with frost. Strange thing, that there could be so much beauty in almost anything." They listened to the rain. "Don't you think?" Yes, this was not a dangerous conversation, Mike thought.

"Naomi, you have always been like this." They looked at each other without talking for a while. "I work with this Japanese fellow," he said, "speaking about bars on windows. He told me once that in Japan they don't have bars in the windows of the psychiatry wards. They just have ordinary Japanese paper screens. He said that all Japanese are so bloody disciplined from early childhood that even the most difficult cases—when they really lose it and, in a rage, break everything around—they still wouldn't even touch those paper screens. How about that?" He looked in vain for amusement in her face.

It was getting late. Mike could see some restlessness about her now. They both knew he would leave soon. Then she told him about the discovery of the gene for the devastating disease her son Ross suffered from, cystic fibrosis.

With increasing excitement in her voice she described the work of several labs in identifying and sequencing the gene. He listened with some fascination, but little understanding, to terms like chromosome-walking and -jumping, southern and northern blots, walking libraries, jump clones, cosmid maps, and exon traps. "I felt, Mike, I should not mess with it, but I could not force the temptation out of my head. I became truly obsessed with the thought of gene-music. It only took a couple of days to transcribe the code of that cystic fibrosis gene into musical notes. There were three base pairs deleted—lost—in that gene, so I replaced them in the musical score by what I thought were the best-fitting notes."

She lowered her voice, now, not looking at him, watching her hands. "The music of that cystic fibrosis gene had such an ephemeral beauty and emotion, Mike, it reminded me of Haydn." She stopped for a while. "And it was of the corrected gene music of my boy's malady, of Ross's disease."

Mike wondered if her hair still smelled as he remembered, the clean smell of shampoo and something else which he could not describe. She still wore her hair the same way, off her forehead. He liked it that way. It fit her gentle fragility.

"Ross, my son, has been sick for years with cystic fibrosis," she continued, "with that terrible disease. It has been destroying him slowly in front of my eyes. That constant, constant cough. Sometimes he could not breathe, could not sleep." She talked slowly without showing any emotion.

She described how she had played the gene music for the first time. It was in the late evening. Ross was asleep already. When she finished, still surrounded by the echo of the finale, she turned around to find her son standing behind her.

Ross asked her to play the piece again, and again. He slept peacefully that night. The next day he wanted to hear it again. Every day since then, she had played the music of the restored gene for him. He demanded that she tape it for him, and then he played the tape daily, as if obsessed, when she was away.

"He never had enough of this music," she remembered. "The score evolves into an affecting tune, a little nostalgic, perhaps. Finally it ends in a waltzing phrase in D major. He always radiated happiness, listening to that part. I cannot ever forget his face, how amazingly beautiful it was, the pain gone from it." She smiled again, her eyes focused on the far away.

Then she told him that Ross's coughing started to improve, that his breathing at night became almost normal. And that his symptoms had started to vanish steadily, and how he was getting better, day by day.

Mike stood up, walked around the bed, and sat down again. He was not sure how to leave now. Song of a gene? He had heard about a bird in Borneo that sings the distinctive opening notes of Beethoven's Fifth Symphony, about singing frogs, and he had listened to recordings of humpback whales singing—and they all share common DNA, common genes. But what sense does it make, what connections? How could the boy have improved by listening to the bizarre gene-tunes of his disease? He felt trapped in confusion—he was in the psychiatry ward.

Mike watched her lips—her upper lip almost fuller than the lower one, the line between them not perfectly horizontal, slanted just a little to one side, not in a sad line and not in a smile. It was strange, he thought. Sometimes her eyes would smile but at the same time her lips would not. He could not kiss her, now. Besides, he knew that she was now talking more to herself than to him. He never forgot her lips, in those years. He remembered every detail, but her eyes—he could not have pictured those eyes well in his memory. Her eyes were green-blue. They seemed distant now. She looked forgotten, diminished in size somehow, far away from the spring outside.

A long silence descended upon both of them, again. Naomi asked him to visit her son, if he could find some time before he left the city, to deliver a letter to him she had written. "And tell Ross I love him." She repeated it. "Tell Ross—give him my love, Mike." He promised to talk to him, to hug him for her.

Outside, the rain that prevents the guest from leaving had subsided. He left her without a kiss. He found the apartment house easily, walked up the stairs to the second floor, and knocked several times on the door with Naomi's nameplate, without response. He turned the knob. The door was not locked. When he entered, the piano music that came from behind the half-opened door down the hallway made him stop and listen for a while. The piano sounded melancholy, the melody repeated in short themes.

He pushed the door open quietly and entered into the bright light. The boy was standing near the window, back to him, naked, just in shorts, illuminated by the sunlight filtered through the tall window, skinny arms, tape-player in hand. The afternoon sun flooded his skeleton-like body. He trembled and shook in intervals, as he coughed. He bent forward, his cough interrupted by strange wheezing sounds, and then spasms of cough, and coughing again.

The melody ended in a waltzing phrase in D major, sounding a retreat for Mike. Soon, all he could hear was the distant cough, and then only silence when he slipped the letter from Naomi into the mailbox downstairs. He started running, escaping over the lawn of the park and, at an even pace, he ran along the cars on the busy street, over the small bridge and across the intersection. He did not stop for red lights. He ran away fast and at a strong pace, never looking back, breathing hard, head bent down.

LOSS OF AN ENEMY

"Life is made of stories, not atoms"

— Muriel Rukeyser

LIFE WAS VERY GOOD. There were smiles, and happiness was on the faces of everyone in the classroom. The air-raid siren sounded like sweet music to them, because it was "preparation" and because it was afternoon. And "preparation"—the long, uninterrupted howl of the siren when it sounded after the noon hour meant that they would all go home and not need to return that day for classes. No more torturing math, no more history or Czech grammar, so incomprehensible to natives and occupiers alike.

Maybe the "acute" would follow: a series of short, undulating wails of the siren, announcing that American planes were actually high above the city, silvery beautiful birds from a faraway unimaginable world, on their way to Germany for a bombing raid. Creeping home from school, the students would be showered with Christmas decorations falling like snow over the alleys and the grim streets and the roofs of ancient buildings, glistening on the grass and linden trees of nearby parks. And free for the taking. Those thin strips of aluminum foil released from the planes were supposed to confuse the radar, but also, Peter was quite sure, were intended to be saved for Christmas—to adorn the spruce, to be scattered over its branches decorated with real candles, candies, and magic glass balls. Even the wire star at the top could be improved by American aluminum.

Today the explosions of anti-aircraft artillery boomed from the distance, and that was good news, too. The artillery had never harmed the aircraft anyway. Twelve-year-old Peter could see clearly the puffs of explosions, well below the planes. But exploding shrapnel was made of handsome material—shining bronze fragments fell back on the city, still hot. Sometimes, with luck, nice pieces could be found, with letters or numbers on the shiny surface. Such a find was of real value. With careful bargaining, it could be exchanged for marbles, even for the yellow ones (but almost never for the glass ones with colored stripes inside).

Peter was not lucky today. On the way home from school there were no fragments of shrapnel and only one small bunch of aluminum strips, which he stuck in the pocket of his short pants. He found the bunch near his apartment house in Marinenstrasse, a peaceful street of unchanging moods and changing but not peaceful names. Before the occupation, it had been known as Verdun Street, after the Battle of Verdun in France. During the occupation, it was named after Marinen—the German Navy.

For Peter it never changed. He knew every single pavement stone there—the few missing ones were in his room. They contained precious fossils such as orthoceras, graptolites, and even part of a real trilobite (extracted from the sidewalk across the street from his apartment). He knew every acacia tree there, having climbed almost all of them for the blossoms, which tasted like honey and were "good for the lungs," as Grandma had taught him. He often wondered how different the trees were from pictures he knew of acacias under Kilimanjaro, shading the olive-colored baboons from the scorching sun of East Africa. The sun was a rare visitor to Marinenstrasse, so the crowns of acacias there were ragged with leaves more gray than green.

He entered the apartment house, closed the main door, and looked around to be sure nobody could see him doing a task he thought to be pretty humiliating. He had to change his clothes fast before being seen by his mother. The hated brown, thigh-high stockings were rolled under his knees and held there with a red rubber band originally intended to be used under the lids of glass containers for canning marmalades and compotes. Now the rubber band went into his pocket, and his stockings were rolled back up under his short pants, where they were attached to the passionately hated garter.

Those indescribable rubber devices for attaching stockings were broken, so the smallest of coins, one heller, had to be used in joining the stockings to the garter. Then he removed his cotton V-necked sweater and pulled it back over his head again, only this time backwards, on purpose.

Breathing heavily after this secret operation, Peter decided to have one more look at the street before going up the stairs to the apartment. And there he was—Hans—just in front of the house next door. Peter's reaction was swift. In a second, the stone was airborne in the direction of the unsuspecting German. He missed him by quite a bit, almost two feet. Since many stone projectiles had left Peter's practiced hand in the past, and since stone-throwing was considered to be one of the very basic, almost primitive skills in the Bubenec section of Prague, the miss by two feet must have been intentional.

"Czechishe Schweinhunde!" screamed Hans, surprised, as his eye caught the parabola of a stone flying by. "Czechishe Schweinhunde!" Czech pig-dog. Swine-dog. What a nonsensical animal, Peter thought. To be called swine only would be pretty offensive, so much that revenge, or better a swift attack, would be required, to maintain some degree of honor—especially if a third person were around. But swine-dog? Czech swine-dog? What to do about the "Czech" part? The "Czech" part made it so much less personal. It made this offensive call just a sort of political, all-encompassing statement, and therefore of lesser impact on a pragmatic twelve-year old's mind.

Hans began his approach. It was a strange attack. The beginning was indecisive, and a careful observer would have noticed hesitancy in Hans's steps. And Peter was a careful observer. He recognized that Hans's attack was a ritualistic response, and thus he responded in a ritualistic withdrawal to the door. The exaggerated and faked expression of fear on his face changed in seconds to an aggressive sneer as pronounced and perfected as only a Kabuki actor could perform. With the sneer, just in front of the door, Peter turned to face the approaching Hans. "So come on, chicken, come on, you shitty coward."

Hans stopped on the spot. He expected to be stopped anyway, his face vainly trying to contort into hate. There they stood, a few feet apart, under a gray sky deserted by the migrating bombers. In the echo of the last howl of the siren, their aggression somehow abated.

The scene did not resemble a Diane Arbus photograph. One might think more of a painting in Norman Rockwell's style, but in a rather grim mood. Their hair had no color, just sort of brownish, washed only once a week, on Saturdays. Their faces had no trace of tan—spring had not yet descended into the depths of Marinenstrasse. Their stomachs longed for a better future—better than dry bread dipped in chicory coffee for a smoother trip through the esophagus, better than daily dinners of mashed potatoes, with chopped onions fried in lard and poured over them for some taste. Two hearts, beating fast now, ready for acceleration. Two brains, seats of two pretty gentle souls, laboring hard on the decision for action, since action must follow this stand-off, and soon.

Many times before, Peter and Hans had performed this routine. By now the rules were well established and were followed with only small deviations. They both knew how "real" enemies should behave. Peter, with the threatening mask still on his face, imitated a mock counterattack; Hans performed a short retreat. And that was enough for today.

In the evening, supposedly doing his homework assignment for school, Peter allowed himself a few pleasant daydreams. He liked the one about the handgun the most. Peter had found a revolver in the bushes of Stomovka Park. Wrapped in oiled cloth, in perfect condition, its white, opaque mother-of-pearl handle and blue steel barrel gave him a feeling of great power and excitement. On the way home, that luckiest of days, Peter had met Hans again in Marinenstrasse.

Hans must have sensed that things were different that day. He had retreated right away to the entrance to his apartment house, with surprise on his face, watching carefully every move of his adversary. Peter's steps were springy. He felt a thrilling feebleness in his knees, though, and could barely suppress the urge to sing from happiness.

He had also forgotten, for the first time, about the rituals, about all the apprehensions and pleasant fears of Hans. Just when he had passed Hans, at a safe distance, as was the custom, he made a decision. As he walked away from him, he pulled the gun from his pocket, looked at it with admiration, turned around, and slowly—as slowly as his control would allow—pointed the gun at Hans, right at Hans's face. Perhaps only a master painter could recreate the expression on that boy's face: not only fear but admiration for the winner, the conqueror—Peter the Great.

Life is so nice, Peter thought, and decided to replay this "movie" in his mind each night before falling asleep—with new variations.

In the following weeks Peter and Hans, the enemies, continued their rites without ever touching each other, repeated their endless offenses without ever feeling offended. They never talked, but they became an important part of each other's daily lives. Peter had to assure himself, often with an effort, that he hated the miserable Kraut. Sometimes he even felt he had succeeded in hating Hans but wished to be more sure about it.

Then came the end of the war and with it a revolution erupted in the country. While Russian tanks roared over the border, crushing the feeble resistance of the Germans, people rose up with an unparalleled excitement.

Barricades dammed the streets, weapons hidden for five years appeared in the hands of clerks, bakers, grandfathers. Smoke filled the air and gunshots and explosions reverberated from the gothic arches of churches, rattling the ancient stained glass windows, killing Germans and Czechs, puzzling children, thrilling teenagers, saddening mothers. Remnants of SS-troops cut breasts off women in the Vrsovice quarter, executed husbands in front of their wives and children in Pankrac, burned the ancient city hall in Stare Mesto. The Czech revolutionary guards shot to death whole families of German civilians forced to swim over Smetena's Moldau, near the suburb of Podbaba.

Peter listened to the news with fear and a child's astonishment. He guarded Marinenstrasse from the window of his apartment, all those days. One afternoon an unknown youngster was crossing the street. Peter saw two soldiers kneel down, and when the echo of gunshots subsided the boy was dead, strangely curled, with one arm reaching in Peter's direction. That evening Peter saw his father being led home by German soldiers with guns on his back, his arms high above his head. Peter's father was an admirable man, strong-willed.

He would never bow to Germans. He would never raise his arms about his head. And yet, here he was, surrendering.

During those four days of the uprising, Peter did not remember Hans. If an image of him flashed through Peter's mind, it was suppressed instantly. There was no place for Hans in Peter's thoughts now. He had vanished.

On the fifth day of the uprising, the Russians reached Prague. At that time in history, they were cheered and welcomed with flowers and joy. They rode in on giant tanks—primitive machines with wood mallets to shift gears. The suntanned faces of the Russians, wide with victory smiles, were admired by Peter and all his friends. The soldiers ate butter, real butter, from one hand and tore pieces of white bread from the other. They drank any alcohol they could get, and when drunk enough, drank gasoline and died. They stole watches, and many wore several on their forearms. In Marinenstrasse, a Russian soldier stole a bicycle from an old woman and was shot to death by his officer.

Another Russian visited Peter's home to everybody's great excitement. He had the expression and the tired, kind manner of Peter's favorite teacher. He showed Peter the worn, tinted photograph of his twin daughters—in pigtails—he hoped to find still at home. Peter liked him because he was a plain soldier and not one of the officers who set a court in the yard of Peter's old primary school. The court was just a long row of classroom benches. There the officers sat, facing the German soldiers brought in front of them. After sentence was pronounced, the German was walked to the back of the yard and shot. Gunfire from the barricades was not heard in the streets and squares any more, only from the elementary school. They were single shots, at regular intervals.

Peter got a piece of real chocolate from his dad's friend. It was dark brown, with an exotic sweetness and the aroma of a tropical paradise. Father and Mother were happy most of the time now, and Peter liked to watch them smile. They enjoyed listening to the radio, which played dance music all day. The acacias on Marinenstrasse bloomed more profusely than ever, and the war was over.

"All Germans must be relocated. All must be sent back to Germany," announced the radio and the newspapers. War is no more; peace will come in the future, people thought. And they moved the Germans through the streets of the ancient city in long processions: bent women, children and old men with eyes turned down, sad suitcases, uncertain steps. Their presence alone disturbed the celebrations. A few infuriated passersby yelled hateful things at them.

Peter knew it was all true about the many unspeakable things done by the husbands of those women and the fathers of those children. So they had to be marched out of the city. Yes, they had to go and never return, to go where they belonged. And he was determined to be clear about this, despite their sad faces and worn suitcases. No, he must not feel confused—not even sad, God forbid.

On May 14, it drizzled all day. It was not windy, but the humid cold made one pull up his collar and warm his hands in his pockets. Blossoms on the acacias hung sadly wet. People were rushing home with thoughts of a warm stove and hot soup. At five o'clock Peter was coming home from Ural Park and wondering where all his friends were. School was out, and there was nobody in the park, just a few insignificant little kids. Near home, In Marinenstrasse, he lingered a while, hoping that somebody might pass by to be coerced into a game of marbles or into planning an expedition to big Stromovka Park. It was still too early to go upstairs.

From around the corner, a procession appeared. Peter knew who they were—he had seen German civilians marching to detention and repatriation centers before. Today, again, they were accompanied by a couple of young Revolutionary Guards with rifles on their shoulders. This time it was a big group, a few hundred people.

They walked slowly, dragging their suitcases and rucksacks, not looking up. They seemed to concentrate on the road just in front of their feet. Their faces stressed the unreality of this situation, this event without precedent in this middle-class, orderly, and pleasantly unexciting neighborhood. Peter decided to go inside the apartment house. He was alone in the street and did not feel enough courage to watch alone.

As the grim procession approached, he changed his mind. At the far end of the formation, something was happening. An older man was gesticulating and shouting. He was not one of the Germans. It was clear he had survived many beers that day, and he was stumbling around, kicking the suitcase of an elderly woman who was barely keeping pace with the others. Peter opened the door of his apartment house and stood there, wanting to go upstairs yet at the same time compelled to watch.

The end of the procession approached, with the drunkard shouting and the old woman still barely holding onto her possessions. Next to the woman walked Hans—shabby jacket too small to fit him, a shawl around his neck, and a cap, a worker's cap Peter had never seen on him before. His head was bent down, staring in from of him, his little boy's body bent to one side to keep his vulcanite suitcase off the pavement.

A light drizzle was still falling on the city. It was getting dark. People were coming home from work now. They did not seem to pay attention to anything. They walked by quickly.

All Peter saw now was the small figure of Hans, framed in the misery of the street, slowly fading away as the procession disappeared. Climbing the stairs he felt a heaviness and an unknown pain in his chest. In his room his scream was muted by the pillow; then it changed to sobs and, finally, the relief of sleep.

It is known that Peter woke up the next morning but that one part of him did not. That part did not die but rather remained alive in his dreams. Nothing is known about the dreams of his enemy.

CHRISTMAS STORY

ON CHRISTMAS DAY we used to go three miles from Prague-6 to Podbaba where my grandpa and my grandma lived. Walking both ways we saved six crowns for the bus and had a good chance to watch the ice on the Vltava River and hear how it cracks. I would have liked very much to jump on one of the ice floes and travel down the river because it was dangerous.

My dad told me stories—the ones about whales I liked the most—on the way. He had never seen the ocean, but had a friend in Argentina. Dad knew about everything.

Grandpa in Podbaba always had a Christmas tree with only a few branches and sometimes they were mostly on one side. Every year on Christmas Day we would go there for goose. Before the gate my father always said, "If you laugh at the tree you'll get one across the lip that you won't believe."

Uncle Prochazka came, too. Uncle Tonda and my dad, they would say he is a moron. When Uncle Prochazka left, Uncle Tonda would always say, "I thought I was going to give him one across the lip he wouldn't believe."

Also, my cousins Mirek and Zdenek came. We played nicely and fast. Grandma smiled a little and said, "Those animals. I'll give them one across the lip they won't believe."

Aunts and uncles and grandparents sat around the big table drinking slivovitz which kids aren't supposed to drink. Usually two or three talked at the same time, but when it came to politics everybody talked at once and waved their hands. It was war outside and when Grandpa said that for sure the war would be over "by cherries" (by the time of the cherry harvest in his orchard), everybody stopped talking. Uncles turned their heads from side to side and aunts turned their eyes to the ceiling. Grandpa had said that about the cherries and the war every year for the four years of the war. Christmas, 1944, he was right.

Grandma did not talk about politics. She only said, "Jesus-Maria, how can you breathe this," because everybody, even the aunts smoked cigarettes with their slivovitz. And the stove, with its inscription "American Heating" under its mica window, added little clouds of soot and smoke to the room.

After we ate the goose, Grandpa was happy. He got the "bishop" every time. The bishop is the ass of the bird and it has two "almonds" inside. They were glands, Dad explained. Grandpa then sat by the tree and smoked a "Virginia" cigar, which had a straw going through it. He puffed powerfully so the tree looked beautiful, as if it were on fire in the blue smoke.

Christmas in Podbaba was very merry, and there were nice presents under the tree, too, like socks. It was a long time ago.

THE CALM SEA

WHEN NAYAK WAS BORN, his grandmother decided that he must not
be nursed and should be left outside the hut to die. The gods had told
her that this is how it should be. He had been born with a deep groove
encircling one of his legs above his ankle, the foot tiny and twisted.
These were the signs the gods had sent to his grandmother, and she
understood. But it was the gods' will, too, that the second day after
Nayak's birth, his grandmother would not wake up from her sleep.

Nayak's mother had started breast-feeding her firstborn, because she knew what had really happened, what was the true cause
of the strangulated foot. She remembered well the time of her preg-
nancy, a night when a group of armed Chinese had landed near her
village on the shores of the Malay Peninsula. It had happened on a
night when all the young men had gone fishing with the big communal
net, far offshore. She remembered every sound of the raid. Every
scream she had heard from her hiding place under the roof. When
morning came and she recognized only familiar voices, she had
climbed down to join the other women in front of the village chief's
house. There, his legs tied tightly above the ankles by a rope, his
arms spread and nailed to the wall, the old chief was dying. She
watched for just a moment, horrified.

When Nayak was born, many months after the incident, she
remembered well seeing the tied legs of the chief. She knew that that
was the true cause of her baby's deformed foot. Everyone in the village understood this, too, but still Nayak was treated differently from
other children. Next to the particular Malayan insanity of amok,
physical malformations were most feared and despised by the villagers.

Thus, growing up, Nayak had often looked for a hidden place
along the shore to be alone. And when he went diving for fish, he dove

without a companion, against the custom of his people. In his teens, he became darker in complexion; nobody knew why. For that, they called him Tamil, after the immigrants from South India. When he reached the age of twenty, his mother died and his uncle took over the house and let Nayak know that he could stay there if he really had to. With that, Nayak decided it was time to leave this village of strangers, his home.

There was a chance to make a good living on Pualu Tioman, an island in the South China Sea. The island had a hotel for tourists. Nayak had learned this from his cousin, who lived there, when this relative had visited the village wearing bell-bottomed pants and a colorful T-shirt and carrying a portable radio. He had been admired by everyone, as a successful man should be, and his words were important. Cousin told Nayak that he liked his foot in a way—it reminded him of the flipper of a sea turtle, he said, and he liked sea turtles best of all creatures. He had given Nayak a present, a plastic snorkel for diving. In his admired bell-bottoms and carrying his radio, he often walked on the beach with Nayak where everyone could see them together. Nayak was very proud of Cousin's friendship, and so he made his decision.

In two days they landed together on Pualu Tioman. That same evening they sat on a soft mat in his cousin's hut, listened to the cicadas, talked, and drank warm beer. The hill behind the hut was covered with dense forest and was so steep that the night-music of the jungle seemed to come from the sky. From the hut, they could see the sea between the coconut palms, shining back in the full moon. The beer was good—so good that Nayak wanted to hug his cousin and all of Pualu Tioman Island.

A smile was still on Nayak's face when he saw the morning mist over the calm water from his bamboo cot. Quietly, he gathered his net-bag with things for diving, broke a couple of bananas from a cluster hanging under the roof, and slithered down the ladder to the sand. His cousin was still sleeping; all was quiet. Nayak thought, "If I do not get rid of that grin on my face it will soon hurt."

He started walking briskly along the sandy shore toward the rocky cape in the distance. He remembered the instructions for reaching the hotel. There, straight in front of the hotel, about a kilometer from the hotel beach, he would see a small island. His cousin had explained everything to him the day before. Around the island he would find a fringing coral reef, and on the outer side of the reef—coral rubble.

Cousin had said, patting him on the shoulder, "There, Nayak, there you'll find tridacna shells. Some are so big that two men can't lift them." He had stretched his arms wide apart, exaggerating the size. "You'll find some good ones on the windward side of the island, in about fifteen meters of water. When you bring them to the hotel, just ask for the gardener. He is my friend, and he will take care of you. You'll make good money, Nayak. Tourists will pay good money at the hotel shop. You'll buy a radio with two speakers. You could even buy me a couple of beers." They had both laughed.

Nayak remembered his cousin's every word and wondered about his new life, his lucky future. "I am a good diver, Cousin," he had answered the day before. "I'll bring up the biggest tridacna shell. You see my flipper here?" He had pointed at his malformed foot. "My flipper will work like the fin of a giant green turtle." They had both looked at his foot, knowing well that it was useless for diving.

But it worked quite well for walking, and Nayak quickened his stride. He left the sandy shore and went through the coconut palm grove, to bypass the rocks. There he trod carefully, watching his way, to avoid the dried palm fronds on the ground. Cobras gathered there, looking for rats that feed on fallen coconuts. The narrow path wound back to the shore through a small forest of black mangroves, some caped with vines. The sun was rising above the horizon now, warming the air, making it pleasant to walk in the shade. Mayak slowed down for a while to watch a gigantic longhorned beetle cross the path. Almost the size of a hand, the copper wings reflected light with a beautiful metallic luster. He rested on a boulder—this time to enjoy the view of an orchid in bloom, its emerald-green blossoms arranged in a single row on the stem like minimal roosters, still glistening with morning dew.

His eyes narrowed against the sun as he descended on an almost white beach of coral sand. A short distance ahead was the hotel. He had never imagined such a large and strange building, such an order to the landscape. The hotel was surrounded by tall trees and royal palms, planted in a pattern. Clumps of hibiscus and bougainvillea, flaming with color, formed a wall separating the hotel from the forest in the back.

Very few tourists visited the remote Pualu Tioman, and it was still early in the day. He could not see any people on the grounds, just somebody on the beach. Cousin had told him that there would be a few skiffs with native men who waited to give tourists a ride, and one of them would take him to the island. But there were no boats yet.

Off shore, over there, was the island. Small, it appeared far away, but Nayak could distinguish the silhouettes of trees. If he swam slowly he could reach it. There were no waves on the sea, and it seemed there was no current in the strait. He reminded himself that there were tridacna shells around that island, and for shells he would be paid money. He did not question what to do. He limped to the edge of the water and sat on the sand.

He noticed two people on the beach now. One was a boy who came running toward him. He was naked and light yellow, just slightly darker than the sand and, despite his child's face, his body was bulky. His hair had no color, Nayak thought, and his big round eyes were strangely pale.

The child stopped nearby and watched Nayak with an expression of wonder. A very tall white woman followed and talked to the boy in sounds without melody. She had no dress on—only a small piece of cloth on her hips. Shyly, Nayak looked at her breasts, which were white and very large. He would have liked to watch the breasts longer but was ashamed.

He must think now about his task. Trying to concentrate, he carefully attached the wooden fin to his good foot with bands made from an inner tube. Then he put on the goggles, with a frame he had carved from soft wood and glass lenses glued in with resin from a euphorbia tree. He rinsed the lenses once in the water and spat on them to prevent fogging. Then he closed his lips over the mouthpiece of the snorkel—the present from his cousin. This would allow him to swim near the surface, breathing with his face always submerged.

After tying the netbag to his rope belt, he entered the water slowly, without a splash. The woman and her boy watched him, motionless. The sea was very calm. Nayak began swimming rapidly but soon reminded himself that he must control his excitement. It was a long way to the island. He settled into steady, fluid strokes, feeling the water gently, not thrashing through it, his good leg with the fin moving up and down in a dolphin-like way, barely making a single bubble or turbulence on the surface. His bad foot moved only slightly, not so much to propel as to avoid creating resistance. It was the deliberate, efficient swim of an experienced diver.

The great visibility surprised him. He could see the bottom gradually slope down, far ahead. Underneath him, clean sand formed familiar rows and shallow trenches, over which the shades of ripples on the surface drew changing patterns, making the bottom seem alive. A school of silvery fish passed under him, now and then rapidly changing direction for no apparent reason. A solitary sea cucumber lay shapelessly on the sand, where it did not belong. This was the sea Nayak knew, the environment where he felt safe and good about himself.

The bottom was rapidly sinking now, and the sand acquired a gray hue. At home, divers rarely swam over such depths, since there was no need for it. The spearing of fish was done in the shallows, between the rocks or coral heads, where both fish and diver could conceal themselves.

When the bottom disappeared, all became silently blue in every direction. This was an unknown world to Nayak. He could easily believe that no bottom existed at all, even beyond the depth he could perceive. For just a moment he imagined himself falling down, which was an unpleasant and confusing feeling.

He stopped swimming to raise his head above the water. The island was still far, the beach closer, and he could still recognize the woman and her boy. He submerged his face again, breathing now through the snorkel with a little more effort, and resumed the swim toward the island. The water underneath changed to a dark blue. Beams of light of different thicknesses descended, changing position, converging nowhere, enhancing the feeling of bottomless space. Nayak felt supported by the columns of light one moment; the next he felt as if he were falling between pillars of light, down into the abyss. But he continued swimming.

Then a solitary Venus lantern appeared close to Nayak, a small, transparent, jelly-creature with tiny fluorescent dots along its gossamer frame. He touched it, and the turbulence made by his hand caused the Venus lantern to somersault. "As helpless as me, now, that lantern in the darkness," Nayak thought, and had to smile. Feeling better, he increased the power of his strokes. Maybe he should think less, and avoid looking around—just reach the island, reach it soon.

Nayak was finally approaching the island when the first shark appeared. It was a great hammerhead, coming upward from the deep, slowly, not directly toward Nayak, looking like a gigantic gray cylinder streamlined to perfect efficiency, emanating power. The hammerhead's head was out of any imaginable proportion, not resembling a mallet—more like a shelf hiding its jaws. Without an enemy in the seats, it was a threat to all those less powerful. With a barely visible movement of its tail fin, it propelled itself away, then disappeared. Nayak had seen the shark with a surge of surprise and a sudden sadness more than fear. But everything inside him tightened. He checked his distance from the island—it was still too far for a sprinting swim, and Nayak knew that he must avoid causing any commotion in the water.

The hammerhead appeared again on the other side. Now it was obvious that the shark was circling, that it might not go away. Movements of its tail were sparse and fluid; the bizarre head never moved even slightly. Nayak looked into the shark's eyes, which stared nowhere, also motionless. There was a remora fish attached to the shark's belly, hoping for leftovers from the hammerhead's feasts. Nayak wished for a companion of his own, too.

He stopped swimming when the shark abruptly changed direction and passed so close to Nayak that he could almost touch it. The shark accelerated and sharply turned around. Its back arched and its head raised up to encounter Nayak's fist—which sent the shark aside. But it returned so fast that Nayak could not maneuver to face it. The feeling was not of a sharp pain. It felt more like being hit with a flat board over his bad leg. His flipper-foot disappeared into the rows of teeth framed in bared white gums. There was no blood at all.

The fish started to thrash from side to side, descending deeper and deeper, effortlessly dragging Nayak behind. The wooden fin came off the good foot. Then the hammerhead detached itself with nodding jerks of its head. Nayak saw that his flipper-foot was gone. Strangely, there was still no blood escaping from the stump.

Now submerged deep under the surface, he felt the high pressure and the coldness of the water. It was quite dark. With astonishment, Nayak became aware of the peace and stillness around him and of no need for breathing, no urge for air. A blacktip shark from the reefs joined them now, passing high above Nayak. The hammerhead came again, from behind.

Nayak's body arched and shattered—arched violently, as if being hit at the waist by an enormous dull fist. His goggles still in place, he perceived himself to be slowly surrounded by a purple cloud, quite beautiful, changing shape, expanding in pulsating rhythms, engulfing his torso like smoke, heavy, yet rising upwards, more and more of it, streaming from his body, as if being fed by a dying fire. Only the remora fish disturbed the purple cloud, gulping at it wildly. Then the blacktip shark's head cut through the cloud baring its teeth.

The woman on the beach, shading her eyes with her hand, observed the silver surface of the water. There was no sign of the strange diver. She took her boy by the hand. The sun was hot now. It was time for a late breakfast—"brunch," they called it, she was quite sure.

A dark papillio butterfly approached the island in flight from across the strait. Almost like a bird, effortlessly, without fluttering, it glided over the still sea, suspended in silence.

ABOUT FATE

THE TRAM RATTLED DOWN the steep slope of Chotkova Road, shaking from side to side in the last turn near Mouse Hole and emerging by the Vltava River. It was still dark at this small hour of the winter morning. The water was black as India ink. Skeletons of poplars glistened with wetness in the bluish beams of street lamps. Vojta stood on the platform of the streetcar, watching, with concentration. He surveyed the silhouette of Prague Castle high on the hill above the river. His eyes would not abandon the castle until the streetcar crossed Manes Bridge.

Vojta's interests did not include historical architecture. Nevertheless, he always felt something uplifting, almost an admiration for that ancient seat of kings of the past and the representatives of the proletariat of the present. He had observed it shrouded in a snowstorm and, on bright days, surrounded by towers and pillows of summer clouds and, at night, lit up as in a fairytale dream. But this morning he stared at the castle without much emotion. He knew he could not afford any excitable feelings—he had to remain a mere cool observer. He must become a master of detachment to survive the future. This morning's ride from home to the Army Recruiting Center marked the beginning of his military future. It was also the end of hope.

The bloody mess had started just about a year ago. Things had been going well for Vojta, a freshman medical student. Friends, girlfriends, and grades were well balanced in his life, which made his days and nights quite happy and allowed him even more time to continue competitive swimming. In turn, success in racing enhanced his popularity with friends and girlfriends and did just negligible harm to his grades. He liked his life and his prospects.

On one sunny afternoon before Christmas, he had received a letter from the Dean's Office. In three sentences, it stated that, according to Law Number 166 of the Legal Code of the Socialist Republic, he was expelled from medical school and all institutions of higher learning. The order was effective immediately. Reading the notice twice, he felt his shirt soaking up with sweat and then concluded he must be a victim of mistaken identity, perhaps a confusion of address.

The next day, in the office of the Referee for Cadres of the university administration, he learned that a few weeks earlier his father had refused to contribute to the North Korean struggle for socialism against the imperialist armies. This deed made father and son enemies of the people. For enemies, there was no place in the university. But there was always a place for them in construction labor forces. For Vojta, it had been the construction of the airfield, specifically: digging trenches and transporting soil by means of a wheelbarrow. From seven to five, on lovely spring days, in the heat of summer, and the rains of fall, together with interesting political "cases" and with so-called "criminal elements," he started to build the Future of Communism. His muscles hardened, and he learned about dimensions of existence he could not have imagined before. He studied life, and lowlife too, while he appealed the decision of the Referee for Cadres and the Party.

With the help of his father, he had appealed to the Medical School Administration first and was rejected within a few days. Then he petitioned the administration of the whole university, then the Ministry of Education. By the end of summer, all these petitions had been repudiated. The only action left was to appeal directly to the nation's president.

There was at least some slight hope in this quite desperate attempt, since the president was known for his unpredictability. In his younger years, in the Kladno steel plant, he had been notorious for being a barely literate accordion player who avoided working with his hands and head alike, but who excelled in inflammatory, and sometimes entertaining, rhetoric at political gatherings of the incipient Communist Party. While his simplicity was often confused with kindheartedness, he still survived the intrigues of the tough pack of wolves in the Central Committee. The powerful aura of his class origins (i.e., vintage proletariat) and his devotion to "the cause" from the very beginning of the class struggle made him politically invulnerable and therefore unpredictable.

On November 9, 1953, the decision to expel Vojta from all universities was rescinded, by decree of the president himself. Vojta had been allowed to complete exams for the second semester of medical school and to continue his medical education, starting the next fall quarter.

In most dictatorships, this might have been a cause for celebration, but in the homeland of Franz Kafka, it only evoked cautious optimism. And indeed, soon after the issue of the presidential document, mail had arrived again at Vojta's door, this time from the Ministry of Defense. In no uncertain terms, in stark military lingo, it stated that the addressee was being drafted for two years military service within a month or two, since he was not, at present, on regular student status. With a new ribbon in the old Underwood typewriter, he had constructed another appeal. It failed to elicit any response at all from the Ministry of Defense. There, telephones went unanswered and entrance was denied, right at the ornate gate of the Renaissance palace which the Ministry occupied.

The tram reemerged, squeaking, onto the bank of the Vltava from between gray rows of apartment houses. On the platform stood the young man in brown warmups with bulging knees, in old tennis shoes, his hair cropped the military way, to one-inch length, against all the trends of fashion of the time. He still gazed at the outline of the castle, barely visible now through draperies of rain. The river beneath, like a stream of lead, seemed to absorb the sky without a ripple.

Vojta smiled. He remembered the planning of the New Year's Eve party. He and Hanus had had to take great care in selecting whom to invite. They both knew that with one bad choice the success of the most important party of the year could be in jeopardy: perhaps a girl who would not drink enough, a guy who would get too drunk, a couple who were going steady. Beverages were plentiful: mostly laboratory alcohol mixed with raspberry syrup, solutions of artificial essence of rum in seventy-five percent ethanol, and a few bottles of Russian champagne for the midnight toast. Games—immoral, amoral, and harmless—were rehearsed and planned in great detail. The party was to happen in three days—without him. But still, he smiled, successful in his resignation over what he knew would happen soon, at the end of the tram ride this morning.

When he arrived at the station by the National Museum, it was still raining. The District Recruiting Center was located at the corner of Washington Street and the Street of Political Prisoners. He recognized it by the row of army trucks on the street. Near the entrance, somebody was struggling with a lighter, trying to light a wet cigarette. It was Hanus. His faithful long-time friend had come to say farewell. They exchanged words and sentences, but what was there really to say? One of the trucks full of recruits departed, blowing exhaust fumes at them. "I'll wait here. Till you come back out," Hanus said.

"Okay." In robot-like fashion Vojta climbed the stairs to the Recruiting Center.

Every kid knows that when a beetle is threatened, it sometimes becomes immobile, rolling on its back, playing dead. But playing anything is a conscious deed, and a beetle does not possess much of a consciousness, we think. The beetle's reaction is an involuntary defense mechanism. When humans are exposed to stress, when tragedy, a hopeless situation, or a loss occurs, the person's senses will sometimes become dulled. Mental numbness often prevails over emotions; primitive resignation overcomes all other feelings. The reaction resembles the protective "playing dead" of the brainless beetle, that master of survival.

On the first floor, Vojta became another shirtless link in the chain of bodies sitting in a state of patient resignation, waiting for their names to be called. One by one the recruits would get up, some with a hesitant smile, or with an obscene gesture made limp by the circumstances, or with a feeble attempt at a careless grimace. Then they would disappear behind a tall door to be examined by the army doctor: Open your mouth, heart okay, liver not enlarged, glands not swollen—and the doctor would motion them, one by one, through another door on the way out to the waiting trucks, their next destination secret. Like pawns in a chess game, when removed from the board, none returned. Vojta waited his turn to disappear.

∾

Bar room philosophers, as well as traveling adventurers, believe that a few times in life one must take fate into one's own hands. In the lives of some, it will never happen; in others, when it happens, the hands grabbing fate might tremble or become too feeble to hold and mold destiny. It cannot be done too often, since common sense tells us that each human being is a cog in the social machine, which punishes deviations. But there comes a time when one must take fate into one's own hands and hold firm.

Another recruit disappeared behind the door. It took longer than the usual five minutes, and nobody else was called in. Then the door opened, and to everybody's surprise the recruit came back—a short fellow, lots of lard on him, and even good-sized breasts. He actually came back. With the widest smile, he raised his arms in exuberance: "I am not going, men. I am staying, men!"

He stood there for a while, putting his arms down slowly. "They found my thyroid fucked. Something about my glands," he apologized. Then he put on his shirt and parka and hurried to freedom without another look at the two rows of frozen faces. For a while, it was very quiet in the corridor.

All of a sudden Vojta stood up without being called, leaving his crumpled shirt, folded parka, and bag with toothbrush and chocolate bar on the bench. He opened the tall door without knocking and entered the examination room. The military doctor sat behind the desk crowded with files. One soldier in field uniform stood next to the door with some papers in his hand. A sergeant, with an unpleasant face, was moving a couple of chairs around. The doctor, bent over the desk, was writing. All three raised their eyes, staring at Vojta with a similar expression of surprise. Vojta did not salute, did not announce his name, and did not stand at attention, breaking three rules of military procedure.

"I'd like to talk to the commander here," he said in an even voice. "About a very important matter." Not a sound broke the silence for a long time, and all four actors remained motionless. Then the eyes of the doctor moved in the direction of a small side door, and his arm followed. Vojta turned, walk to the door, and, without knocking, entered.

His shirtless torso was pulled tight and his face was a controlled mask. A few measured steps brought him in front of a giant desk. Behind it sat the colonel, veiled in a blue screen of cigarette smoke. There were a few coffee cups on the edge of his desk, and another officer was leaning on his elbows on its corner. A couple of high-ranking officers were smoking, half-stretched out on the sofa. The atmosphere was casual, as goes with early morning coffee and cigarettes. Nothing much happened at first when Vojta entered, but one might have detected curiosity on the faces of the officers and astonishment on the face of the colonel.

Without delay, Vojta told the colonel that, first, there had been a mistake in summoning him to be drafted this morning, since he was a student at the university (a lie, actually). Secondly, their error was grave, since Vojta had a document to that effect, at home. His half-naked stature, in an at-ease posture, now also encircled by a blue stream of cigarette smoke, appeared almost ghost-like in this bizarre setting, like a scene from a surrealistic movie—a movie with an unhappy ending, no doubt. "There was a mistake made, Sir, Comrade Colonel." The uncertainty disappeared from his voice. "I cannot go. I cannot be drafted today."

The colonel made an attempt to rise but sank back in his chair, staring at Vojta with a puzzled expression, not anger. Vojta stepped closer to the desk. "I have all the necessary documents. I am a student at the university. I just came to tell you this, to explain why I am going home now, Sir." There was no response from the colonel or the other officers. Vojta straightened up slowly, as with effort, his voice now loud, having only a slight tremor. "Goodbye," he said. He still waited for a response which did not come. "That is all. Goodbye."

Vojta finished these few sentences, wrote down his full name on the back of an envelope lying on the desk—with the colonel's pen—and left, without asking permission. Before he reached the exit, he could hear the uncertain voice of one of the lower-ranking officers from the sofa. "We will investigate. We will investigate this."

Soon Vojta walked into the rain again, with Hanus's arm around his shoulder and his hand on the nape of his neck. Vojta's hands were still holding firmly to his destiny, of which he had taken command about ten minutes ago. Waiting for the tram on Wenceslas Square, he argued for buying additional white wine for the New Year's Eve party—and Hanus agreed. They realized that one girl who had been invited preferred white, and they had almost forgotten to plan for it in all the commotion. It stopped raining before their tram arrived.

Vojta was never contacted by the army again. This is an historical fact. It was considered a miracle—and, as it is with miracles, it remains unexplained.

COLLECTOR
OF LIGHT BULBS

FROM AN AERIAL VIEW the chain of islands called the Florida Keys looks like a string of emeralds in the azure plane of the Caribbean—jewels with inclusions of settlements and the bridges connecting them. In the middle of May, the royal poinciana trees bloom incredibly red, as if their crowns were perpetually on fire, and Jamaica dogwoods (still leafless after the dry winter heat) cover themselves with light gray blossoms resembling styrofoam and never move in the wind. Then, after the first rain of the coming wet season, the thatch palms shoot new spikes of leaves skyward, and the glossy bark of gumbo-limbo trees shines, brick-red, to justify the local name of "tourist trees" (since they remind some of the sunburnt skin of visitors from Minnesota).

It had been almost twenty years since the tourist had spent a vacation in the Keys, and he remembered it well, as if it happened yesterday. He remembered the places where he had been diving, fishing from the bridge . . . and the food, too: the key lime pie, the turtle soup, conch chowder, and fried grouper (his favorite).

This May he wandered again through Hemingway's house in Key West and withstood a Papa Double with two jiggers of rum in it at Sloppy Joe's Bar, rubbing elbows and shoulders with other tourists. Later that evening he found a cozy-looking bar well off Duval Street, with only a few visitors in bright T-shirts with colorful pictures of coral reef fish. "Development, AIDS, and drugs, my friend," his companion at the bar told him in a conspiratorial whisper, "coming from all over the Carribean."

He ordered another couple of Coors for both of them. His companion waited for the bartender to move away, then stretched his arms like a fisherman describing his catch, and whispered, "Bales of *ganja* like this." He then ordered a shot of dark Bacardi and turned it into his beer mug. "Every night, man," and took a gulp with obvious satisfaction. "Things are dangerous on the Keys. Everything is changing for the worse." The old Conch was getting more pessimistic with each new round of Coors enriched with the dark Bacardi. Slowly his head bent lower until it rested, motionless, on the bar.

The next morning, the tourist left the crowded southernmost settlement of the U.S. for a scenic drive north. He planned to snorkel on the Gulf side, somewhere near one of the many bridges, then spend the night on Grassy Key. But first, he had to stop on the beach on the Atlantic side of Big Coppitt Key. He was looking forward to visiting the place where he had spent a few nights camping, years ago, where he used to look for washed-in mahogany boards.

It was difficult to find that place. There was a new road across Big Coppitt, but finally he located the remnants of Old Barbara's shack, which he remembered was near the beach. Old Barbara used to sell bait, Coke, chips, and candy bars there. Even here, off the main road, there were new houses with pink plastic siding, and developers were scraping the land to bare coral caprock, for still more building lots. He recognized the beach. There was the white sand strip. Parallel to it stretched the narrow but dense belt of red mangroves, and behind them the salt pond, full of water in high tide and half empty when it was low.

The beach had changed, too. It used to be clean, just some seaweed and clumps of turtle grass washed on it, and pieces of driftwood and a broken lobster trap or two. He used to find a few mahogany boards there, always wondering whether they fell from a ship or were carried here by winds and sea currents, all the way from Honduras. Now there was plastic everywhere on the sandy beach—plastic bags, pieces of polyurethane foam, plastic bottles of all kinds, tangled pieces of nylon rope, a solitary condom here and there, odd rubber thongs. The look of it pained the tourist's heart. But at least he was finally alone. There was nobody around, as far as he could see—just a beat-up Datsun truck with a topper parked at the beginning of the beach.

It was a curious vehicle. The back gate was opened, windows down. Inside, one could see a pile of blankets, containers of different shapes, beer cans, and pieces of clothing. And in the front, there was barely space for a driver to squeeze in. On the roof of the topper was attached a big doghouse with a chicken wire door agape. When the tourist approached, he understood why the owner could have left the open pickup unattended. Tied on a long rope (fortunately) a German shepherd charged, baring its teeth without a sound.

Giving the dog the widest berth, he passed it, walking down the deserted beach, stepping over debris, trying to avoid the occasional blobs of asphalt. It was high tide now. He inspected every board washed up on the beach, cutting into some with his knife to see the color and grain characteristic of mahogany. It was a beautiful knife with a rosewood handle and he kept it razor sharp and cradled in a handsomely worn leather sheath. But none of the boards showed the deep red, close-grained structure of the prized wood which, when polished well and soaked with linseed oil, would appear almost iridescent and feel like velvet to the touch.

Just before the beach ended, a man suddenly stood up from behind a sea-lavender bush. He was naked, which was not obvious at first, since he was suntanned evenly, his shoulders the same dark hue as his buttocks. The tourist overcame his hesitation and continued walking, trying to look preoccupied with the junk on the beach. When he got closer to the man, they greeted each other and exchanged a few meaningless phrases.

The man looked at the tourist intently, never averting his eyes during their conversation. His rusty full mustache matched the color of his hair, which was quite long but not all the way to his shoulders, and was smoothly combed backwards. His liking for the sun was obvious, not only from his deep tan but also from the complicated map of wrinkles and creases on his face. Because of this, it was difficult to judge his age—maybe fifty or even sixty. His voice was youthful and clear, and he talked quietly, without any accent. The tourist complained about the litter on the beach, expecting to strike an accord with the man. But he did not seem to be of the same opinion.

"Yes, there are a lot of things on the sand. I find many bulbs here, mostly after a storm," he said, turning to the beach.

"You find bulbs?"

"Electric bulbs, light bulbs, *mi amigo*," the man explained. This "*mi amigo*" puzzled the tourist for a moment, but he was more curious about the bulbs. The collector of light bulbs seemed to be interested in the conversation, since he continued without further questioning. "I collect them—light bulbs, you see. From all over the world. You can find them on the beaches everywhere in the Keys." He paused. "And this is a good place, here." He looked at the tourist, apparently curious to see his reaction. The tourist obliged with an expression of wonder. He was intrigued, indeed.

"That is very interesting. You are a collector of light bulbs, then!"

The man moved a few steps away and, from behind the sea-lavender bush, he brought up a light bulb. His physique was quite impressive for his age. No fat on his flat belly, his buttocks were firm as an athlete's, and he moved with surprising fluidity and ease. He was not circumcised, and his pubic hair was the same rusty color as his mustache and the hair on his head. He handed a bulb to the tourist. "Read this," He pointed at the faint inscription.

"Osram?"

"Yup, Osram. From Germany, all the way from Europe," the man said, stressing "Europe." "I have them from all over. Some must be thrown out of ships, like the Asian ones."

"Oh, really?" the tourist encouraged him.

"From Japan, Korea, and Singapore. You see, those from Asia have inscriptions in red. They are a rare find, they are," he continued. "I got bulbs from Poland and Mexico, too, and Canada. Yup, from Poland, too." He seemed quite impressed by the Polish specimen.

They talked more. The man explained that, on some light bulbs, the identification had been smudged off by the sand and that he had discovered a way to read it well, under a fluorescent light. "I take those to the library in Key West and read them there. They have fluorescent lights in the library, you see."

Like prehistoric pterodactyls, a flock of brown pelicans hurried by, on the way to their night perches, their wings almost touching the calm water. And the first night-biting mosquitoes announced themselves. The shadows of the two men elongated to the edge of the water as the setting sun touched the twisted tops of the mangroves behind them. The bulb collector pointed to the sun with a gentle but slightly theatrical movement of his arm. He smiled a pleasant smile, and the tourist recognized the hour as late. He left, feeling a sympathy for this quiet man. He wished him the best of luck in his hunt for more exotic light bulbs.

After walking for a while, he turned around to wave. He was surprised to see the collector watching him with what appeared to be powerful binoculars. After he had carefully bypassed the parked pickup truck and the watchful dog, he turned around once more. He could still recognize the reflection of binoculars pointed at him from the distance.

∾

In his motel on Grassy Key, the tourist discovered that his knife with the rosewood handle was missing. He was sure it must have slipped out of its sheath when he was bending down to pick up a board on the beach at Big Coppitt Key. The moon was almost full. There was plenty of light on the shore, so he left without hesitation hoping to find his knife. On the way back to the beach, he was thinking about the strange bulb collector.

To his surprise the truck with the doghouse on its roof was still on the beach when he arrived. After locking up his car at a safe distance from the truck, he started to walk, feeling some wariness. To avoid the German shepherd, which he suspected would be on guard with even more vigilance at night, he entered the bush of red mangroves which separated the beach from the salt pond. After stumbling long enough to bypass the truck, unseen, he ventured back to the beach . . . and instantly crouched down. Somebody was there and not far from him. A man in a black shirt and dark pants stood motionless, watching the sea.

Soon he recognized a small boat with two men pushing it silently through the shallow water to the beach. He felt the bites of mosquitoes and no-see-ems but did not dare to shift even slightly. Anxiety made it difficult for him to breathe. He regretted intensely leaving the safety of his motel room. The boat approached the beach.

"*Aqui, aqui! Rapido!*" the dark man on the beach exclaimed. There was no hush in a voice used to giving orders. It was a command, not an instruction. The dark-clad man still did not move, but the boaters hurried. One jumped into the knee-high water, while the other handed him down a cube-like parcel which reflected the moonlight on its plastic wrap. For its size, it did not appear to be heavy, since the boater waded with ease with it to the shore. He placed it at the feet of the dark man who apparently supervised the action.

The boater hurried for another load while the tourist watched with increasing anguish from his hiding place. He remembered, now, the bearded customer in the bar in Key West sayings, "Every night they bring the *ganja*. Bales like this," the bearded Conch had said to him the day before, stretching his arms. A dense cloud of mosquitoes buzzed around the tourist's ears, and tiny no-see-ems penetrated his T-shirt and pants. He felt his face swelling with bites, but somehow he stopped registering the pain of the stings. They were still bringing more parcels to the beach. Only the splashing of water by hurried men disturbed the silence of the moonlit shore. It was low tide now.

The tourist breathed in a mosquito. He could feel it, deep in his throat, which constricted violently. It felt like being grabbed. He could not inhale. He tried to remain motionless despite the shattering sensation. He felt increasing dizziness, and the spastic pain in his throat did not subside. He covered his mouth with his hand and tried to breathe out. Then his lungs exploded in a single, gurgling bark.

The boatman with a bale in his arms froze. The dark man remained standing, without movement, still facing the sea. Silence ruled again. Then the dark man turned around with lightning speed and dropped to the ground. The tourist could see him creeping rapidly in his direction, in the fluid motions of a predator.

Without thought, the tourist sprang up and ran. He sprinted, full speed, straight into the narrow belt of mangroves. He crashed through the tangle of roots and low branches wildly, stumbling but still keeping his balance, feeling no pain. When he emerged on the muddy shore of the pond, he turned sharply to his right, dashing into the soft mud along the mangroves. He ran hard in the wet silt, which reached above his ankles. He felt like flying, briefly hopeful, amazed by his speed. He turned his head—and saw only his tracks in the mud, glistening in the moonlight, and nobody behind. He did not decrease his pace when he reached the shallow channel running from the salt pond to the beach through the swath in the mangrove belt.

Then the dark man emerged from the mangroves. The collector of light bulbs, breathing heavily, stopped his pursuit and watched the running tourist. Then he turned around and retreated into the mangroves. He knew that the running man, in about ten paces, would reach the area of quicksand.

HURRICANE

The dead volcano's
chilly surface—and also
wild strawberries.

Having a fatal disease,
how beautiful my fingernails
over the coals of charcoal!

— Dakotsu Iida

THE POWER WENT OFF right after the announcement of the hurricane's eye at 24°6' degrees latitude and 81°4' longitude. That was still a few miles off shore, just about on the reef. The voice of the weatherman was controlled, business-like, too cool, perhaps. After all, his radio station was at Key West and they had already had gusts of over seventy miles per hour. US-1 was barricaded by fallen trees on Stock Island. Planes were piled up at the airport.

All of Pelican Key was under water, except for a small elevated section next to the sinkhole by the western-most point. That area was thought to be an ancient Indian mound, Caluza Indian.

Erik's house was on lower ground and did not fare well. It was constructed almost three decades back, before county building codes and federal safety rules required building on stilts at least ten feet above high water level. Erik had it set on wooden pillars massive enough, but only shoulder high. They served as an imaginary protection working more against the crawling critters of the tropics than against the hurricane surge that now flooded the house.

The house resisted the wind force at the beginning of the cyclone, since all the structural wood was oversized and tied, by skilled imported craftsmen, to the enormous forty-foot long central beam that supported the cathedral roof. Erik had had the beam, solid Douglas fir, shipped all the way from Oregon. It was carried from the road to the construction site by thirty slender Cuban refugees hired in Miami, all in identical tennis shoes donated by Centro Cubano. Heavy machinery was avoided to prevent the trampling of even a single botanical specimen of the "hardwood hammock." That is what the native mini jungles are called in the Florida Keys.

A few minutes after noon Erik Lance Bauer stood by the bookshelves observing the lowest row of his collection of first printings, half-submerged. The house itself trembled, creating ripples on the water reaching to the knees of the old man. Waves were peeling off the gray back of the binding of The Cantos by Ezra Pound. The Cantos—that was ages ago, years before Emily, even The New Cantos was before her. He pronounced her name aloud, but not loud enough to be heard over the howls of the hurricane. Emily. He had not known any other prayer for several decades and it was time to pray now. Emily, he whispered again.

A crushing sound reverberated from the bedroom, then a heavy thing, a tree branch perhaps, ripped into the shutters of the library. Erik decided to move to the inner bathroom, which seemed to be the safest bet for survival. He gave one last look at his books, and then at the south wall, with its series of Picasso engravings and the one Chagall he owned. If the house goes, he pondered, that one will be lost, its existence unknown to the history of art. It was a rare painting from the master's Vitebsk period. Never mind that Chagall's daughter refused to authenticate it—he bought it from the painter himself.

On the opposite wall, he kept only one painting in a simple pine frame. A dot of a fishing boat nearing the horizon, leaving a Norwegian fjord, a dreamy sort of watercolor by Emily Ruzicka. His eyes lingered on the painting for a long while. Then he waded away, holding on to the shelves.

He built the home away from his family. The farthest away he could determine from studying a map of the continental United States. As far away as possible to escape his family's constraints, to get outside the conventions of those gregarious folk. He himself built his own solitude. He was well aware of it. His independence, and more, had been taken care of by a generous trust fund and, later, by the inheritance. I have never worked a day for money, he used to proclaim with conscious arrogance in his younger days, and with a tone of regret, perhaps, in the lassitude of the last stages of his life.

On the day of the hurricane, Erik L. Bauer seemed much aged for his seventy years. He had felt the decline with more confusion during the past year. His steps had become uncertain. And lately his mind had become increasingly forgetful.

More and more the past had become a refuge to him, sheltering him from the present, a cheerful sanctuary. More often his thoughts had been going round in circles, with himself at the center. He had been finding that tropical solitude harder to bear—finding the infinity of the emerald Caribbean sea and the azure sky *ad perpetuum* bringing just dreams, nothing more.

He found only a few alternatives to the solitude of his shelter. There were excursions to the raw oyster bar near the park of trailer houses. There were affluent neighbors, kind people in his and hers Bermuda shorts and individual small hats, who often referred to the Florida Keys as Paradise or "a little slice of heaven." They revered Erik. His appearance had been a valued asset to any party—long white hair, features suggesting intelligence and learning, and wrinkles that could have had their origin in a decadent past or simply in exposure to the Caribbean sun endured for decades. They admired their neighbor for his oddities. His use of English puzzled them pleasantly, and sometimes his sarcasm or irony awed them. They were intrigued, too, by his total dismissal of the importance of finance, since they had all worked long and hard for their millions (no old money on the island). They secretly rooted for their old man when Erik would would answer a newcomer about his line of business. "My line has been retirement. Since the age of one."

It was rumored that women sometimes arrived from the airport to stay with the bachelor for days. Where they came from remained a mystery discussed often and in hushed voices. Were the acquaintances of Erik's from his yearly trips abroad? What did they come for? To the old man who had to stop in the middle of a staircase to recover his breath, while faking interest in the view of the garden or a carving on the banister? Those lucky neighbors who stole glimpses of his visitors all agreed that the women looked "foreign" and were of different ages. The hair of the last one had been cut to one inch. The one before that had had a single braid—she must have been no more than twenty years old and looked "different," an observer reported. All the neighbors knew that Erik would not evacuate for a hurricane. He was "different," too.

Before hiding in the inner bathroom Erik surveyed the situation. On the lee side of the house he tried the door knob. The door was sucked open in an instance, creating a whirl of water that almost took his legs from under him. Holding onto the casing, he peered out. A red polystyrene buoy, torn from a lobster trap, flew by horizontally in a spray of foam and mangrove leaves. A cassuarina tree, which he had been planning to have trimmed for a long time, split in front of his eyes with a cannon sound and half of it crashed into the palm grove. Palms were bent as if made of rubber. The driveway was deep under water. Surreally, waves with white caps rolled on the driveway toward the road. His garden of orchids and bromeliads no longer existed. He recognized some of his rare vines plastered on the wall of the garage as a tangle of leafless ropes. He retreated, leaving the door agape and vibrating in the wind.

Erik made it to the bathroom on trembling legs. He climbed on the tank of the toilet, put his legs on the seat, and balanced precariously above the muddy water. Some seaweed squeezed in under the door. He was cold and fatigue kept him motionless. The train of the apocalypse roared with steady vigor outside. Thumps of branches crashing into the house sounded like blasts of shotguns in a successful hunt. Suddenly, the clean tone of a trumpet penetrated his ears, then drums, and a French horn sounded a wind-powered symphony never recorded before. The beautiful sound of a flute slowly climbed the scale. The wind instruments prevailed in the music of the hurricane. Erik listened and a smile appeared on his face.

He leaned back on the wall behind him. His eyes closed, freeing him for the voyage back in time.

∾

It happened about four decades ago. He had met Emily on the shore north of Trondheim, on one of those crisp sunny days which startle Norway in the fall. It would have been surprising to encounter anybody on the the coast near the fishing village of Hopen, since the tourists mostly flock to the established fjord circuit near Bergen or to the mountain treks past Lillehammer. The shore near Hopen was out of the way of any traffic, except for the rare local settler looking for stray sheep, or as a destination for a forbidden rendezvous of fisherfolk from the village. That day Erik had decided to find a deserted place to make a picnic for himself. After two days of Trondheim he wanted to own the North Sea privately, determined to let himself be enchanted by the sound of the swells washing the shore.

After parking his rental car near the village pier, he looked in vain for a pub or a store to buy a bottle of beer to go with his sandwich. But this was not Europe proper. His disappointment faded soon after he found a path out of the village and disappeared behind boulders the size of nearby houses. Between granite outcroppings he crossed a springy bog fed by a spring gurgling from under the stone in the shape of a sheep. He waded through a growth of dwarf willow and foot-high birch, slid down the smooth rocky wall, and then—the view of the sea.

She was standing against the sky on a flat rock above him and facing the fjord. Her straw-colored braid, hanging long to her waist, flowed over her windbreaker. She was concentrating on her painting and could not hear his steps hushed by the moss.

Afraid to startle her by his sudden appearance, he cleared his throat. Her paintbrush froze for a moment, then she turned to him slowly. The features of her face muted him. It took him a long time to recall the Norwegian greeting.

"God Dag," she answered, paintbrush motionless in her hand. Erik felt at a loss. He had exhausted his Norwegian vocabulary in his greeting. "Do you speak English?" he asked finally.

That was the moment he saw the first of her smiles, and he remained speechless. He did not realize what the gods knew already about the love at first sight of Erik Lance Bauer and Emily Ruzicka.

She was an American on vacation, staying in the village for a week, painting the sea every day, lonely sometimes and now happy to meet somebody who spoke her own language, she said. Soon they shared the sandwich, drank from the nearby spring, talked about her watercolors, and about the paintability of the fjord and the impossibility of painting the sunset. The orange discus, inclining toward the western horizon amazed them by the speed of its disappearance. Then they parted, promising to meet on the same flat rock above the fjord Erik had come to view alone.

On his return to Trondheim, Erik lost his way to the ferry in Rorvik twice, and was already worried about losing her, too. He realized his foolishness but he could not calm his mind. In his hotel, after only a few wistful hours of sleep, he awakened in the darkness, dressed, and waited for the sunrise by the window. Staring at the harbor he saw only her smiling face. When she smiled, one corner of her lips was slightly higher—he remembered that clearly. It was strange that her brittle smile did not match the expression of her eyes. They did not narrow into a smile, they expressed openness, candor, or sincerity, he thought, which was not altered by amusement. He could not remember exactly their color, which bothered him, but he was certain he had never seen a face like hers, beautiful like hers. Emily.

They met again above the fjord on the flat stone near the spring. She painted the fjord undisturbed by his attention. The sea was marked by a silvery ribbon drawn by a fishing trawler, which caused her difficulty. He watched her clean forehead creased by concentration and became sure he must be the favorite of Destiny. They walked to the shore after she finished. He helped her over the rock and their hands remained together. They did not release this hold until they came back to his car.

The road took them around the baldheaded mountain with a waterfall falling silently into its own rainbow. Driving through pine and spruce forests she pointed out mushrooms of gigantic dimensions. "My ma would never leave this place till all were safely in a basket. Boletus, hribek." She wondered why nobody picked this rare delicacy. They tried to pass a herd of well-fed cows sauntering down the middle of the road, their teats full. But the animals panicked and ran alongside their car, splashing milk all the way up the windows. Emily was much amused—Erik was embarrassed. They surprised a moose by a small lake. The waterweeds hanging from its snout did not diminish the majesty of that motionless advertisement for pristine nature. It is possible they both thought about embracing one another at that moment. Erik almost reached for her.

Then the unpaintable setting sun ordered them to separate. He had to leave for Oslo. She would stay a few days longer to finish the painting of a red fishing boat leaving the fjord for the open sea. He did not kiss her—she was too beautiful—he just put his hand on her braid and slid his palm along its length, looking into her eyes. He would remember those eyes now, the blue-green irises—like the fjord farther from the shore when the sun is in the noon position. Pretty color on the pure white of the eyes.

Alone in Oslo, Erik woke up every day long before sunrise, surprised by the intensity of his confusion and longing. During those nervous days, he revisited the Edvard Munch Museum, imagining her next to him and talking to her in front of each distressing painting. Walking the streets, he whispered to her about characters passing by, made up strange stories about them, as if they were trolls of a bizarre fairyland. He thought about her every waking minute and dreamt about her every night in dreams which loitered in his mind all day.

At the predetermined day and hour, they met on the stairs of the Palace. When she saw him across the street she waved, then ran to him. She looked stunning with the city in the background. Gracefully long waisted in creamy pleated slacks, the fashion of the time, her tan sweater tightly on her slender chest, her endless neck in harmony with the single braid descending to her waist and reflecting the Northern sun in golden hues. She gave him a kiss, a fleeting kiss which surprised them both and prevented conversation for what seemed an eternity to Erik. They held hands as they walked through the village-like capital of Norway, by now his favorite city.

In Cafe Ethiopia she told him about her stay up north, about her Chicago family, her Slavic origins, her midwestern college.

He told her that he came to Norway to visit the family of his father's new wife, a woman who, before the death of Erik's mother, had been one of their maids in Oregon and his father's lover. And whom Erik liked the best of his relatives, by far. He did not tell Emily that he had never worked for money but did tell her he was a student of English literature. Instantly he felt stunned by his lie and confessed it, with sweat erupting on his forehead. It was an awkward moment. She withdrew her hand from his and it took an hour for their communication to improve. Then she accepted his invitation for dinner at his hotel. "The only place in town with an edible menu," he assured her. Leaving the cafe he noticed, with pride, that she attracted the admiration of all the guests, ladies and gentlemen alike. They parted with some hesitation.

For dinner Erik dressed carefully, rejecting several alternatives from his wardrobe, including a carnation in the lapel. Finally he left his suite in a dark woolen blazer, white linen shirt and a silk ascot of conservative pattern. He parted his chestnut hair precisely and ruffled it on the temples. The mirror satisfied him that his handsome face hardly gave away his age—he was fifteen years senior to the dazzling young woman.

She arrived on time, radiant in a blouse of dusty rose color with a spray of pink pearls around her neck. He told her they were otherworldly. Touching them, he realized that they were artificial, and then he became unsettled by the fact that he even paid attention to his find. He was determined to admire everything about her and to reward her beautiful existence by the dinner-perfect night.

The dinner was made easier by Erik's acquaintance, the head waiter. He was the oldest employee of the hotel and he attracted Erik's attention by his unusual expertise in all culinary matters, by his eel-like fluidity between the tables, and by his peculiar habit of whistling thinly an unrecognizable melody, so faintly that one could hear it only in closest proximity to him. His brilliantined jet-black dyed hair was parted in the middle, and his complexion was so white it appeared blue. He and Erik took great pleasure in communicating with each other.

"Sir," the whistling waiter whispered and bent down to Erik's ear, "just a few hours ago, Japanese Matsushima oysters have been delivered to the Hotel Grant. The greatest oysters in the world, as you must certainly know, sir." He nodded slightly to Emily. "They came on a fast ship from Stockholm, having been flown directly from the tanks of Sendai, the nearest city to the archipelago of Matsu-Shima."

"Oh, really, my friend," Erik responded with an expression of surprise. "From Matsu-Shima? The pine islands, where they have been artificially raised to achieve the length of eight inches at least—twenty centimeters, you would say." They both took delight in this way of speaking. Emily observed the room.

"Pleasure to serve you, sir, madame, indeed." The waiter bowed slightly with approval on his blue face.

"One dozen. Lemon only. Please," Erik ordered.

For the main course Erik and the waiter conspired on langustas in dry vermouth sauce, but Erik requested the replacement of vermouth by sake to honor the Japanese provenance of the oysters. For dessert: whole unripe walnuts aged for a year in brown sugar and cognac.

"No lefsa or lutefisk, Emily," he pronounced with self-satisfaction as he adjusted his ascot. With langustas, against the rules, the wine he ordered was red—Hotel Grant stocked only one of the Premier Grand Crux, by chance the one that Erik admired the most. The Chateau Latour would surprise her, he was certain. Not exactly the smooth perfection of Rothschild Laffite—but a rowdy complexity which changed with astonishing speed when decanted.

"Get ready for this, please," he gestured with excitement. He held up his wine glass. "The world of science, Emily, has not the slightest notion about the chemistry of this phenomenon." She nodded and pointed out the arriving guests she was sure were the U.S. ambassador and his wife. "How ambassadorial looking, isn't he, and look at her blouse. Wow!"

Emily refused the oysters but liked the langustas, dessert, and the famed wine which she judged as "really good, if a little strange." Seeing Erik's expression, she said that he was so much preoccupied with food that he might get fat. Then she laughed and leaned her calf against his leg and put her hand on his and smiled at him. The warmth of her hand disturbed him. She laughed often that evening.

Most of the guests left. She asked him to lend her a book to read and suggested going with him to his room to pick it up. She admired his bedroom while he selected a few titles for her.

Then he called a taxi and accompanied her to her bed-and-breakfast place. The city lights gave off a cold blue light. Almost nobody walked the streets. They watched the passing houses without words. She thanked him for the dinner, shook his hand, and disappeared into the house. Back in his hotel he lay on the bed repeating one word, many times: idiot, idiot. At three in the morning he woke up from a restless sleep and sat by the window, waiting for the sun to rise. Then he ran.

He lost his way and in a state of panic found her house by mere luck. She opened the door and without a word let him in. She was just wrapped in a towel and her wet hair was flowing in streams smelling of lavender soap. She emanated the warmth of her shower. She embraced him and looked at him for a long time. Then they kissed with passion true lovers know. He carried her to the bed, lay her down gently, and looked at her face again, trying to absorb her. "I love you." He said these three words for the first time ever, since his sense of honesty had prevented him from making this promise to any of the women in his past.

He had to force himself to close his eyes to make love to her. So beautiful she was.

Then they lay still, holding to each other. A feeling of happiness filled him with such an unexpected intensity he started to laugh. He became aware of only her and himself with her, nothing of the past and nothing of the future. Laughing, he looked through the ceiling into his heaven.

His laughing alarmed her, and she sat up in uneasy surprise. He assured her, first, that he was a simpleton and idiot, then, that he was the happiest man in all the world.

"Emily," he explained, "in Inuit, the Eskimo language, to make love is translated as 'to laugh with the woman.'" He sat up with her and cupped her breast with his hand. "Can't you see the depth of the meaning? Only the happiest love will fit the Eskimo term, the loving of only true conspirators in friendship." He did not wait for a response. "I think it must beat, hands down, any passionate passion, any torturous torture of love—to laugh with each other, to. . . ."

She put a finger on his lips. "You use so many words, Erik. You do, and I like it, Erik. But right at this moment you know what I want to do with my Inuit?" She pulled him down to her. She did not laugh saying it, but broke into a smile, with her eyes partly closed in an expression of intrigue and conspiracy. A streak of hair lay over her chin. From her body it seemed as if ". . . sudden rosy smoke was rising"—a verse by Yusuke Keida flashed into his mind. He wrapped her body in his, tightly.

They showered together for a long time in a bathroom with warm pinewood walls and ceiling on which the vapor condensed into drops fragrant with resin. He licked the drops from the wall and the dew from her body. Of thirst and hunger he assured her, and proposed making her breakfast.

"The greatest meal Frenchmen ever invented!" He dressed in a hurry and jogged out onto the street like a kid, bursting with energy and barely controlling the urge to sing. Back in her room he saw with satisfaction that she had already put a clean towel over the table and washed two glasses from the bathroom. She confessed to her curiosity about the best food Frenchmen ever invented. Erik pulled a morning fresh baguette out of the bag he was carrying. He cut it along its length into two halves and with his Swiss Army knife spread unsalted butter on each. On it he layered malosol caviar a quarter of an inch thick, the best from the Caspian Sea. The glasses he filled with cool, inexpensive riesling, tinted lightly yellow.

"Genius of simplicity, Emily, my love!"

She liked it, he saw with delight. With caviar on the tip of her nose and on his chin, they ate hungrily and drank. They talked silly—what a discovery for Erik. Then Emily told him she loved him, too.

They kissed with mouths full of those sturgeon eggs salted and smoked to perfection. They sipped the wine with slurps, spilling it on their naked chests and without showering curled together in sleep.

They slept at any hour those days and nights, and made love simply and in complex gymnastic exercises. She proudly called it their loving orgy. He insisted on a term from the Inuit language. That was their only argument. He believed he had climbed clear out of the hole of reality and had fallen—in love.

"To make love to you, Emily, is like breaking fresh village bread, with its heavy crust and heavenly smell and its soft insides. A taste so delicious that one cannot describe it," he told her, and soon was on his way to the nearby liquor store.

"Grappa! Here you are. The simplest distillate of the Italian peasant. Drunk with the breaking of village bread!" They drank and made love with enthusiasm and altruism, and often.

She also praised the grappa and drank it straight. And she laughed at the idea of bread and loving. He embraced her behind and kissed it since it was pleasingly out of proportion to her slenderness. "Come up here, Erik," she called. "Up here, close to my soul. And kiss me." She believed that the soul rests in the brain and could be easily shared by the kiss of lovers. Grappa made it easy for him to accept her belief.

They danced to his whistling, watched in disbelief the people on the street hurrying about instead of making love. They handfed and groomed one another, compared the darkness of their nipples and the luster of their nails. Erik told her many things, and she listened—most of the time.

He became sad only in the moments he realized, with increasing clarity, that it would be impossible to attain the emotion of these extraterrestrial days again. She was never sad. "I love her," he assured himself. "I love her." Time acquired a peculiar quality: the hours and days and nights became progressively shorter and shorter.

When the date arrived, Emily decided that they should say goodbye on the street. There he stood steady, his lips in a contortion of a smile. She held his hands. He had to be the one to walk away not looking back. He managed that on that street in Oslo. But he had looked back ever since. He wanted to believe that it was with true love that he loved her. He knew he worshiped his love for her and the small watercolor of the fjord he carried home with him.

Erik Lance Bauer was awakened from his past by the complete absence of sound. From his toilet tank throne he stepped down into the water and walked away on uncertain legs, holding on to the walls. He could not pry open the main entrance door. Above, the main structural beam, the one carried in by thirty slender Cuban refugees, was sloping down at one end.

He could barely get through the kitchen. The water there was covered with floating garbage. He managed to push out the kitchen door leading to the back deck and instantly became blinded by the light. The sky was ultramarine blue, without a blemish. In the cypress door a large splinter of black ironwood was embedded as a warning arrow. A collapsed lobster trap was wrapped around the only standing post of the deck's railing. The railing of the "widow's walk," blown off the roof, was leaning on the stump of the pigeon plum, like a ladder. The sad remains of a pelican, his favorite pterodactyl of the islands, floated near his knee, half-submerged, stripped of most of its plumage, the pouch under its beak flopping in the water like a rag.

For decades Erik had been living surrounded by greenery. Trees, ground cover, even the sea was green when the northwestern wind blew. Now there was not a spot of green anywhere. Not a single leaf in the forest of splinters and skeletons of trees.

Erik understood the situation. He was in the silent center, the eye of the hurricane.

"The eye is looking at you, kid." He forced a grimace and looked up to relieve his eyes of the desolation—only to see an event which filled him with emotion. Hundreds of birds, voiceless dark silhouettes, soared against the blue. There were several species, all together in a large circle with different rhythms to their wings. Some were gliding motionless. All were hiding in the eye of the hurricane. When the eye disintegrated they would all be destined to smash into the waves or on to the land. They would all perish violently, he knew. But now, in the eye of the hurricane, the birds were one big community, with hope in each of them.

Erik tilted his head backward, stretched his arms apart, and flapped them slowly, up and down. Again and faster. He felt as if he were lifting up. Just a few inches. But would they want him to join them in their last gala flying performance, these magnificent frigate birds, these royal terns and kingfishers? They would laugh at this crow, this scarecrow, this fragile, spindly marabou. He longed to go with them, even to share their fate, just not to stay here alone, as always. He tried lifting his wings again, feebly, but tired soon. Streams of tears mixed with the salty wetness of his face. His hands rested on his heart.

The rising breeze made him shiver, and then a sudden puff of wind. The hurricane's eye was moving away. He could see the black wall of clouds on its fringe moving in. It would just be a few minutes before the sheets of rain and the wind would return, their force increasing rapidly to a hundred and fifty miles per hour or more. This time the wind would come from the opposite direction to complete the destruction.

Erik waded back to the shelter of his bathroom where he managed to close the door behind him. The screams of the hurricane increased rapidly. The gunshots of breaking wood announced the beginning of the symphony of wind instruments, deafening the old man who again held on to the tank of the toilet.

He observed his legs, hairless on the shins and around his ankles, pigmented spots, skin loose and shriveled where muscles used to bulge. His bony hands were spotted, too, and his fingers were bent and knobby. But his nails were still beautiful—pale, milky, opaline, fluorescent in the darkness of his cave.

Erik found two new companions in his shelter. A pair of gecko lizards was attached to the ceiling. He had always felt a kinship with these ghosts of his house. In the evenings they amused him by wiggling across the bedroom ceiling, moving their hips like Caribbean whores at the beginning of the night. Geckos also worked the night shift, catching a stray mosquito with a sudden surge of speed, or dining on a confused moth attracted to the lamp, licking their lips with pink tongues afterwards. "*Tres faciunt colegium*—we will make a hurricane party of it," he forced a cheer.

Suddenly, with one powerful gust, part of the ceiling tore away and was sucked up violently. With it went the two pale geckos. At that moment, for the first time in his vigil, Erik was overwhelmed by a feeling of indifference to his survival. To hope seemed fanciful, the inevitable became irresistible.

But it was the last of the great screams of the hurricane. The apocalyptic train outside departed to the Gulf, the forte of the symphony unrecorded before changing into moderato. The water level subsided, and more light came in through the missing roof. It was all over.

Erik slumped slowly to the floor, into the corner. He bent down his head and embraced his legs. He rested his forehead on his bony knees in a peaceful, fetal position. His breathing was slow, in the rhythm of a sleeping man. He closed his eyes, opened them in wonder, and closed them again. His eyelids were the only moving object on all of Pelican Key.

He drifted away. There were shadows all around him, moving shadows he had to avoid. He flew through them into the clouds of brilliant dust, like millions of stars in all directions. The speed of his flight increased until all the stars fused in a bright-lit space. He recognized it as an ocean stretching to the horizon.

Then he saw her. On the big flat boulder above the fjord, waiting. She was smiling, her face unchanged. After four decades, not a single crease, not one wrinkle on her pale complexion. Her lips were full, the upper a little fuller than the lower, as he remembered. Erik could not make a sound but felt his tongue and lips form the words he had often dreamt he owed her. He wanted to ask many questions and say pleasing words to her.

"I have been waiting, Erik," she whispered. "And you came. It is time to be with me now, my love." She stretched one hand to him, palm upwards. That was her way—when reaching to him she always held her palm up.

He shivered when she locked her fingers with his. She led him carefully between the great boulders down to the sea, on which the waves were motionless as if frozen. They walked so lightly they seemed not to touch the ground. Silence ruled the space around them. The only sound came from somewhere in the wreckage. It was the high-pitched buzz of the seven-year cicada calling to all who might have survived the hurricane on Pelican Key. The white head of the old man lifted slowly and turned, his ear searching for the direction of the insect's mating call.

GOODNIGHT, TERRY NIELSEN

MISSY, YOU WOULDN'T HEAR a shotgun go off right next to your pretty ears," the fat man in a checkered shirt behind the counter told her with a wink. He handed her the sound prevention ear muffs. She positioned them over her ears and in an instant was deprived of all sound. Moving her head from side to side she was surprised by the completeness of the silence.

She was the only woman in the chain saw shop. The other customers in checkered shirts gazed at her, and the lips of some of them moved. The attendant moved his own lips back at them. He looked at her, speaking, and pointed at the ear muffs. She smiled, satisfied, and removed the muffs.

". . . the saw going and hold it straight," she heard him finish, whatever he started.

"I'll buy it," she said, too loudly, and shook her hair to tidy what the muffs had undone, hurriedly paid and left the strange place—Chain Saw Sales and Repairs—to make it home before rush hour. She used to slow down driving home, taking pleasure at looking at their house on the corner of Jamaica and Ideal Avenue, at her pride of green lawn with the flame bush by the entrance. But she hurried now. Running into the kitchen, she got liver sausage ready for Chuck and some chips. He should be home in half an hour. "Shit, I forgot the beer." Luckily, there were a couple of cans in the back of the fridge. He always had to eat the moment he came in and gobbled everything up within minutes.

She unpacked the ear muffs, pulled her hair back, and put them on, adjusting the fit carefully. How strange, she thought, to actually hear the hum of silence. Somehow her vision seemed more acute, things around her looked sharper. She stood by the sink, watching the soundless drip of the faucet.

She screamed when hands grabbed her waist from behind. Chuck's laughter roared when she tore the muffs off her ears. His expression of satisfaction and the smell of beer on his breath brought her back to reality. Nothing was said when he stopped laughing. After he finished his sandwich, he asked her about the "idiotic ear muffs or whatever."

"Got them in a chain saw shop. I'll try to sleep with them." She looked away from him. She ceased to simulate affection a long time ago and had lately become unable to simulate conversation. There was too much hostility.

"It better work. I am getting fed up with you. One day I'll pack my stuff and that's it, I'm telling you," he mumbled, switching on the TV, one hand on a beer, the other changing channels one by one and then back again. That was his routine, seldom varied, unchangeable.

&

The dog had been barking every night for at least a month by now. She could see it sometimes, two back yards away in a chicken wire enclosure, pacing from one corner to the other, like a caged leopard. It did not make a sound during the day. The first barks started around eleven o'clock at night. A sharp, cough-like bark—then quiet for a minute, then bark again, then silence and bark again and again, till dawn. She would turn in bed, covering her head with the pillow, trying to imagine beautiful things, thinking about how it was before Chuck, picturing her parents' house in the San Fernando Valley, with the big fig tree leaning against the garage. She devised mind games, counted silly sheep to the hundreds. Sometimes she almost made it, feeling the sleep coming, numbing her body—then the barking. She began to anticipate the sound when the pause between the barks became longer, getting even more alert.

After the first week of sleeplessness she called the police. They promised to talk to the owner of the dog. Nothing changed. She went to the police station and pleaded with the sergeant—he assured her that things would happen, but nothing did. She tried to plug her ears with cotton and developed an earache—while still hearing the barks. She walked like a somnambulist during the day, dreading the night. Her fatigue became constant and almost painful. Then Beth, her best friend, who moved to the town from the northern part of the state, advised her to buy the sound protecting ear muffs. Up north, Beth told her, everybody has a chain saw. They know about these things. They chainsaw from childhood. She also described what the chain saws do to their hands, legs, and other parts of their bodies but how only the simple guys get deaf because they think ear muffs are for sissies.

When she went to bed, Chuck was already unconscious, sprawling on his back and breathing deeply in a sleep which nothing could disturb. His eyes were partially open, showing the whites. His mouth was also open. His belly looked like a wide-spreading tumor, she thought. And growing too. When he had told her today, for the thousandth time, that she would see his heels some day soon, she wished she could scream what she really thought about him at that moment, what she longed for in her daydreams. He lay there in bed like something heavy being hacked by a chainsawyer gone mad. It was certain that he would rise again. She used to cry, but not any more.

She looked in the mirror while she undressed. Good. Then she put on the ear muffs. They fit well when she lay on her back. It impressed her again how instant was her descent into complete silence. She was about to fall asleep for the first time after sleepless weeks, when the ear muffs slipped off her ears. A sharp bark jolted her, a flame of heat shot to her temples, and sweat covered her in an instant. Another bark. Breathing deeply she took control of herself and adjusted the muffs. But they would slip off again and she would lie there with her eyes closed, scared of her helplessness.

When the twilight of the morning drew lines between the shutters, she got up on uncertain legs, her hands shaking. She sat down in the kitchen and did not make her usual hot chocolate or breakfast for Chuck. When he appeared in his crumpled underwear and again screamed about leaving her, bitch, she sat calmly, her hands not trembling any more. Soon after Chuck had slammed the door behind him, the morning sun flooded a corner of the breakfast table, making the pattern of the flowers on the tablecloth come alive with bright colors. She made hot chocolate in the big mug and took a long time to finish it. Finally, she felt at peace when she made the decision, a decision with no alternative but success. So far she had failed with the barking. Thus, she must prevent the dog from barking. She was going to kill it with poison.

∾

This time she was the only woman in the Western Gun Shop on Ottertail Avenue. The other customers withheld their remarks when she bought the Subversion Sling Shot. The seller explained, in a loud voice (so everybody in the shop could appreciate him), about "the improvement in stability due to a handsome arm brace and unheard of accuracy of the weapon." He stretched the sling.

"The sling itself is made of polylatex, not rubber, ma'am—very powerful for small game huntin'." He put a serious frown on his forehead and managed a deeper voice. "I do not recommend it for use by children and very young adults." She paid $12.99, politely refusing steel pellet or marble-type ammunition. On the way home she stopped in the grocery store for a pack of wieners.

At home she removed one wiener from the pack, cut it into three pieces, and shot them at the pen of the dog two lots away in fast sequence. She missed every time, once hitting the branch of a tree, and overshot the pen twice. The dog in the pen did not move.

It became obvious she had not resurrected her old skill in sling shooting from childhood.

She realized that to deliver a poisoned piece of meat into a small dog pen over the distance of two back yards, between trees, would require careful planning and training. She had seen children on the neighboring lots on occasion. For this reason, she knew there would be no margin for error, for a miss, no space for hurried or emotional action. Moreover, she started to feel a little sorry for the dog and was glad she did not see him very clearly in his pen.

When Chuck came home the sling shot was hidden in the garage. She dutifully served him the sandwiches and beer—right under his nose. Still, he yelled at her again and the tension built up. Later she watched him fall asleep in a chair, snore, salivate, and finally stumble to bed in his work pants, his billfold sticking out of his back pocket. That night the dog barked again.

It was the fourth week of sleepless nights for her.

At ten o'clock the next morning, when the neighborhood was at its quietest, she divided a wiener into three parts, one and a half inches long each. Concentrating hard, she stood on the spot she marked on the concrete in the backyard. She stretched her left arm and pulled the sling shot to within ten inches of her eye. The powerful pull of the sling caused her outstretched arm to shake slightly. She steadied it for a second and then released it, actually seeing the projectile accelerate between the branches of two oaks and descend to the target. It hit the outside of the wire fence of the pen. The next shot she aimed a little higher, stretching the left arm fully and pulling the sling to exactly the same length as before. The wiener landed in the pen and she could see the dog approaching and bending to it. She felt exhilarated and—maybe because of that—she missed the third shot. Of the next three attempts, one was successful.

Her results started to improve and by the end of the week two out of three shots landed reliably in the pen; a few times even three of three would bring her hope. She knew it was still not good enough so she doubled the number of attempts, shooting four series of three pieces every morning. At the end of the second week, three of three landed in the target area with only two misses in the last four days. She became confident of making the final shot of a poisoned piece after another week of training. During those days she managed to get a few catnaps, which kept her going.

At ten o'clock on each of these last few days, the dog would be waiting for her. He would stand watching her in his pen, wagging his tail, expecting a wiener. It was a pretty dog, she thought, kind of a shepherd mix, with a face that looked like it was smiling. She would have liked to have a dog that could make a smiling face. It gave her pain around her heart to see it wagging its tail like that.

But still, every night the dog barked—every sleepless night.

ᖇ

She got the poison from Beth. The cyanide came from the chemistry lab at the hospital where Beth had been working for the last year. White powder. Beth explained what would certainly happen to a child who ate it in a piece of meat. They both got emotional talking about it and cried.

∾

In the morning stillness, soft air moved just the leaves on the top of the oak. Unnoticed by her a cardinal's call accentuated the calmness of the early summer landscape of the backyards. She stood again on her mark, not feeling too good, with the metal instrument in her outstretched arm.

Since breakfast, she had thought about her grandmother, her dad's mother, who grew up and then died alone on a small farm in southern Minnesota. Of many images and memories, the one about goat kids was the most poignant. There had always been a few she-goats on the farm and after mating with a smelly billy goat from Mr. Larsen's place, they would give birth to two or three kids. They were the friendliest and the most playful animals of all. Grandmother used to take special care of them. Often she took them into the kitchen, hand fed them, and cradled them on her lap, one by one, so there was no injustice done. And sometimes, when nobody was around, she got down on all fours on the floor and played with them—at seventy years of age! She gave them pretty names, too.

And then she cut their throats behind the barn where nobody could see what she did or her crying either. That's how it was meant to be, because, on the farm, kid-goats were born to be eaten on Easter. It was not a rule of religion or law of nature, but kids were always eaten on Easter on the farm.

Since early morning, she had been thinking about her grandmother and the goat kids and the dog that had to be killed. She thought she knew what grandma would do with a dog who prevented her from getting a restful sleep night after night. She wished she could be sure, though.

With a precision which amazed her, she was now depositing the pieces of wiener right into the middle of the dog pen on all of her last training attempts. She decided that the last, the fatal shot, would be delivered on Friday morning at ten o'clock. On Wednesday, two days before that final shot, she practiced once more. All three shots followed an identical trajectory. Before the final attempt, which she pretended was the poisoned one, she felt a rush of adrenaline. But she repeated her movements exactly and the third piece landed in the center of the pen. She would be successful on Friday. She knew that for sure.

On Thursday, the day before that critical Friday, she met Beth for lunch at Perkins, near the shopping center. It was a nervous lunch. Beth looked and acted worried. They talked about fashion and about Beth's buying a used car. But both of them knew they were avoiding what was most on their minds as they parted, each with an obvious excuse.

Just before she pulled into the driveway, Chuck's pickup was leaving in a hurry. How strange for him to come home this early, she thought. And why was he leaving in such a hurry?

In the bedroom things were strewn about all over the place. The drawers had been opened, his clothes were gone—even all of his shirts—and his gun rack was empty. His pillow was gone too. He used to go hunting a few times a year, and a couple of times he went to visit his brother in Dakota. But he had never taken his pillow with him before.

She took her shoes off and sat on the bed, feeling hollow in her stomach. Not crying. Not celebrating. She just sat there shedding the heaviness of her thoughts. She put on her Bob Dylan favorite from at least ten years back. She replayed it a few times, and with each change she felt a little better. When darkness came she walked lightly into the bathroom, washed, put on the extra large T-shirt she'd kept from high school days. Coming back into the bedroom, she stretched out on the blanket and sprawled her legs over both parts of the king-size bed.

Before the smile disappeared from her face she had fallen deeply asleep. In the morning she woke up late, opened the window and slept some more—till Friday noon. Later she called Beth and told her about Chuck's leaving and about her sleep. Beth sounded ecstatic when she heard that the cyanide had been flushed down the toilet.

∾

"Hello . . . yes, this is Terry Nielsen." She paused a moment on the telephone. "No, sergeant, I don't know if the dog still barks. . . . Yes, maybe it does, but I just don't hear it . . . It's okay. Thanks for calling anyway. Bye." After she'd hung up she filled the dish with dog food and put it by the door.

Terry's new puppy, a boxer with a pudgy nose and a face that often smiles, loves to be hugged and has the reputation for being a good sleeper. Sometimes the puppy howls. But it is a milk and honey sound, soothing, mellow, like her name—Maya. When Terry goes to sleep, Maya is already ahead of her in dreams on the other half of the bed. There, sometimes, Terry would hold her paw.

Goodnight, Terry Nielsen.

THE BEST TIME IN LIFE

IT FELT ALMOST LIKE SLOW DANCING with an unexplored high school date. That good. I was walking again through the West African jungle, in the morning, moving lightly in my shorts and thin shirt, not a drop of sweat on me but soaking in everything around me. The freedom was tangible. After the night rainfall, the humid air took the scent of orchids and sweet jasmine well. The bamboos sounded music powered by the light breeze. The golden shafts of light between the canopy of trees and palms changed patterns, making everything around me appear in motion, alive. I sensed the biology in every blade of grass and fern edging the path, even in the pebbles strewn on the red laterite ground. It would take an hour or so, Joseph had said. No sweat. So I stopped often, looked around, listened, smelled.

Near the creek, a foot-long millipede crossed my path like a shiny brown train, and the rainbow-colored agama lizard greeted me with vigorous pushups meant to impress. It was a male, of course. A display of shining jewelry glided above my head—iridescent morpho butterflies, glossy wasps, even a rare-sized buprestis, the jewel beetle, buzzed in a straight line above. I noticed a group of fruit bats, hanging like wet pouches on the branch of a slender afara. They have been passing over my house in Nunugu every evening, making inimitable sounds, but nothing like the barking—despite their resemblance to miniature Dobermans. They are my friends.

Strange shrieks from the shadowy undergrowth and the increasing staccato of an unknown bird halted my steps. Then silence again. You want to either sing or think in the holy green stillness after a night rainfall, so I rested by the mute creek that spread over the path into a shallow ford, compelled to think about big things, Nature, the Creation. But I had to go.

It was a rainy season Sunday morning and my destination was the village of my acquaintance Joseph, where he lives with his wife Amadiume. Joseph is a technician in pathology at the Nunugu Hospital. We talk often because he likes to practice his English and I like to learn more about him. Like most of his tribe, his manners appear gentle and his speech is always measured and quiet. Unlike many of his countrymen he looks directly at your eyes when speaking and his smile is always at the ready. Recently, he gave me a nice bowl made by Amadiume of the fruit of the cannon ball tree. I will give him my Bowie knife before I leave. I looked forward to meeting him in his own environment, in the place of his forefathers, and I suspected it would be a significant occasion for both of us.

Approaching the village I passed the burial site, recognizable from the scattered clay pots for sacrificial offerings. I was curious to inspect them, but I was in a hurry. A young couple crossed the path in front of me, holding hands by their pinky fingers only, according to local custom. A woman approached with a bundle of firewood balanced effortlessly on her head, the tightly-packed baby on her back swinging its head impossibly back and forth in a peaceful sleep. Then the first hut appeared, surrounded by orderly rows of yams and coco-yams.

It was my first visit here, so I was unsure about what kind of welcome to expect. But my hesitation disappeared when a crowd of naked children with umbilical hernias swarmed around me, their eyes wide open in amazement at my paleness. Joseph must have been alerted by that mysterious African telegraph, since he appeared within moments of my arrival to save me from this crowd of little people. In a flowing toga (not unlike my grandmother's nightgown) and embroidered skull cap, he looked more distinguished and taller than he did at the hospital. He shook my hand without squeezing it, released it with a ceremonial swing, gave me a friendly smile of welcome, and led me to the square.

The important elders had already gathered in the men's house. They greeted me with the customary limp handshakes and somber sentences I did not understand—with stateliness, without deference. The frailest of the sages motioned to me to sit down on a clay ledge worn smooth. It was the place of honor. Then the men talked quietly among themselves, paying no attention to me, since only women and children show uninhibited curiosity toward strangers. I watched the faces around me with interest. Each one was sculptured differently, in varying hues of brown, none disfigured by deposits of fat, the skin taut over their cheekbones, the whites of their eyes red, the creases and wrinkles in various configurations of seriousness. None of them carried a necklace of the dried navels of their enemies. Perhaps they had left them home for my visit. None wore a goat's heart on his neck (the heart of a virgin had been forbidden by the colonial administration a long time before), so there was no way to recognize the chief.

I lit a cigarette without asking permission, since a small display of arrogance is expected from a white man (and, frankly, I craved a puff), and when followed by friendliness, it helps to establish a mutual respect—not unlike in the boardroom of an American business. And the "board members" in front of me were not much different either, except for two phenomena: the mean weight averaged fifty pounds lower and the posture of dignity was maintained with a natural ease.

I smiled politely when an old woman brought a gourd with palm wine. Joseph explained in his amiable accent that the palms had been tapped yesterday at sunset and the village tapper had collected the juices this morning before sunrise. This way there would be less quantity but the wine would be fresh and cool. The tapper is an experienced man. With some apprehension I asked if the wine had been diluted with water—as is usually done—and learned that it had not. That pleased me no end. I could avoid this dilemma: either I could drink and get sick like a dog or not drink and offend everybody in the men's house. Palm wine is an almost sterile fluid, self-fermented by its natural yeast only. But when water is added, it comes from a creek or pond, thick with such a variety of bacteria, amoebas, and other pathoorganisms (responsible for the fifty percent child mortality here) that an unaccustomed visitor, drinking watered wine, unfailingly ended up with diarrhea or an even more serious ailment. Having seen, in autopsies, bags of yellow mash in place of livers as a result of amoeboid infection, I took the news of undiluted wine with barely disguised pleasure and thought of the customs of this village with respect. And the wine was pleasantly cool, with the taste of bread and the scent of Urquell beer from Pilsen. It made the morning committee of biblical sages smile and talk with increased vehemence.

Joseph translated the few formal questions of the *ozos*—the elders—about my occupation, country of origin, domicile, and state of health. Then I distributed my spare pack of Benson and Hedges. With solemn bows and handshakes Joseph excused us and we left to visit his house.

Our way was circuitous so that we covered much of the village. Joseph delighted in soliciting the admiring looks of his peers. Young ladies giggled. Their erect elegance and brown beauty has never ceased to stir my postpubescent fantasies, and I wondered if it could be confirmed that they put the biting boatman bugs on their breasts to swell and enlarge them. An old woman approached us and Joseph translated what she said. She asked me to stay with them in the village permanently. If I didn't agree, she would steal me. She roared with laughter. Her pitch-black face and negroid appearance aside, she bore a striking resemblance to one of my old aunts. I wondered how that could be possible.

An emaciated woman, stark naked, ran across our path with arms above her head, and, farther on, an older man, grimacing wildly, forced me to accept a palmful of coins. These were insane people, victims of a cerebral form of malignant malaria known to readers of romantic colonial novels as "blackwater fever." I assured an embarrassed Joseph that all was well, that I understood they were ill—because only the insane would display bodies no longer beautiful and only the insane would give money to a white man. Joseph and I understood one another perfectly.

Joseph's house did not have a thatched roof but distinguished itself by corrugated sheet iron. This "progress" is the price a successful man with a job in town has to pay for his eminence. An iron roof, in contrast to the "barbaric" palm-thatched one, creates heat in the house which is often difficult to bear. The mud walls of his house were nicely hand-polished with only a few cracks, and the half door was made of the traditional, simply carved iroko wood. Bending our heads we entered with greetings.

Inside, the beam of light from one of the two windows flooded his wife Amadiume as she sat on a metal cot. She startled me with her beautiful face and peaceful smile and shy eyes. Her hair was done in tiny braids that met in a complicated pattern at the top of her head. Her complexion was a warm brown in shade, lighter than Joseph's, and smooth, without a wrinkle. My thought was to wonder why Joseph would plan to take a second wife, as he had confided to me in town. On the wall above her head hung a framed picture of Christ.

Amadiume was very pregnant with a girl to be born in just two days and to be named Ifuome. My mental photograph of this scene is titled "Waiting for Ifuome," and I can still recall it clearly in every detail, any time.

She got up with graceful effort, greeted us in her language, and brought cola nuts on a saucer advertising Cinzano. It is an honorable custom to offer a cola nut to a guest. We dipped the nut segments into a very hot paste—a variation unknown to me before. Then Amadiume said something to Joseph and he explained that she would have to leave us to visit her younger brother who was recovering from a bad scorpion bite. Judging from the way Joseph looked at her wobbling away, I knew he would be a good father to Ifuome. Amadiume parted with a smile so warm I wished she would stay.

I looked around the room. "You have a nice place here, Joseph," I said as I sat down on the "kitchen" stool. The mud floor was swept clean and the clay walls were polished smooth. A wooden stand had a saucer and a few cups neatly arranged on it, and a pole spanned a corner on which hung European clothes and a couple of sparkling clean shirts. In poverty cleanliness is the highest virtue, and neatness is a sign of good upbringing. Both are signs of a long pedigree.

"We try, Prof. There is not much money, you know."

"Your wife is expecting. It is good you have the job in the hospital," I said. "And the war is over."

It had been two years since the end of the Biafra-Nigeria war, and the country was slowly getting back on track.

"It's good to have the job. I only wish it paid more."

"Did you have a job during the war, too?"

"Now I have a few coconut palms and the yam field, with my father," he said.

It appeared that Joseph didn't want to talk about the war. So we exchanged several polite phrases and talked about farming for a while. I did not want to make him uncomfortable, but I needed to know.

"At least we have peace now," I said. "And the war is long over."

"Ya, peace. It is good to have peace now."

"In that war, you were a young fighter then, Joseph, weren't you? On the Biafra side?"

"For two years," Joseph said, shaking his head. "A long time and much hardship, Prof, much hardship."

"Were you fighting around here near Nunugu, or down south?" I asked. "I've heard it was more difficult down around Port Harcourt, in the Niger delta. Lowland forest, lots of disease, malaria, and such."

"I fought around here, but at the end we retreated to the delta. That's where I was stuck when it all ended."

It was a vile war. Villages and towns were wiped out, thousands of women and children were massacred, and thousands died of starvation. Atrocities were committed on a mass scale and were so barbaric one can not bear to think about them. It was typical, sadly, for the sub-Saharan part of the continent. It solved nothing and helped nobody except for a handful of "big men," and it was soon forgotten. I have heard some about it and read much, too, but never talked with a fighter before. I did not want to appear too eager, though.

"Wars go on all over the world," I said. "I just hope it was the last one here. Forever."

"I don't know, Prof—not even the elders have much hope."

"What was your function in the army, Joseph—artillery, tanks, or what?"

"We did not have any tanks, had no airplanes, nothing like that. Nigerians, they had all that. They had everything from the British, you know. We were fighting with rifles. I got me a repeating revolver, too." He looked around the room, as if somebody might be spying on us. I believe he almost told me he still had it hidden there.

We chewed on a piece of cola nut. It showed its stimulating effect pleasantly. His eyes seemed brighter and he helped his English with his hands, pulled at his robe often.

He continued. "Maybe you would say reconnaissance—that's

what I did a lot, because I grew up here in the forest. We would slip through enemy lines, spy on their positions and numbers. Took prisoners sometimes, too." I nodded and Joseph continued. "It was dangerous, but me and my friends, we knew the forest. Not like those Hausa or Fulani from the north. We could move like forest spirits."

"I can imagine," I said, "like juju spirits, invisible."

But Joseph did not like me to use the word "juju." His face showed it and he stopped talking. I offered him a cigarette.

"We had cigarettes and plenty to eat at the beginning of the fighting. We got cans from Sweden, with meat and fish in tins. Very good. The cigarettes—when they got wet we did not dry them, just threw them away. Just like that." He smiled and paused.

"You were a big man, Joseph."

"I was a big man."

"Like the chiefs are now?"

"Oh bigger, Prof. I could do anything I wanted. Anything, when we came to an enemy's village, anything, Prof."

"Powerful weapons?"

"The best U.S., best Italian. You know Bereta? Very good and beautiful."

"You were a big man, you were," I said, pushing it too much, maybe. "You had some good times, too."

"Oh, ya, Prof, good times." A smile crossed the still youthful face of my friend. "But bad times, too, mind you," he added hastily. "Very bad war."

We sat quietly for a while, looking in different directions. Some children peered through the door and Joseph shooed them away, almost angrily.

"Like once, down in the delta, west of Port Harcourt, we made camp on a creek, with a lot of catfish in it. We did not have much to eat by then, but we would not eat the fish. Dead bodies up the creek, women, they had bellies cut open, you know. Fish was no good to eat." He asked me for a smoke and continued. "As I said, it was in the delta, a bad place even in peace. In the evening, the men returned from patrol. And they told me about my cousin, Okonkwo. He was named after his father." He paused, staring at the floor. "You see, Prof, we were more than brothers. We were always together. Best friends, like donkey's teats, always together. They told me Okonkwo was dead. He got lost and when they found him, his soul was gone. His head was gone, too." Joseph took a deep breath and looked at me while turning his head from side to side.

I turned my head, too, and we became silent again.

"Just as they were telling me about my cousin, the other group of soldiers came from the forest. They had prisoners with them. I don't know how many. Some were just kids, spy kids, you know. Naked and smeared with palm oil so that when you caught them they could slip away." I gave Joseph my last cigarette and lit it for him. "I became so sad, Prof, so sad about my cousin. He was like my brother, I told you."

"Yes, I can imagine, Joseph."

"I was so sad I grabbed a zap gun and mowed them down. Those prisoners. All of them."

It was getting late and I knew I should not wait for the dusk since it would not be wise to return through the forest in the darkness. I wanted to thank Joseph and get going, but slowly. We finished the last cola nut with that hot relish. Joseph was sitting on the bed with Christ above it. But he was now staring at the opposite wall, his mind somewhere south of here, in the past, I guessed.

"The war," he said quietly as the smoke came from his mouth. "That was the best time in my life. Ya, the best time, Prof."

"I know."

We shook hands limply, as is the custom here.

LAKE NAIVASHA

THE LEGENDARY SUNSET occurred without anybody noticing. Three six-packs of Kenya's "Tusker" beer did good to all and nobody minded its temperature, which was the same as a mild breeze of a tropical evening. Because of the singing, none of the six heard the dying of the day, nobody noticed the change in the tunes that the cicadas played in the giant umbrella of an acacia tree above them.

The fire flames projected six happy silhouettes on the parched grassland around the camp. Girls approached dangerously close to the heat of the flames and tossed away their sweatshirts, laughing. Guys looked into the eyes of the girls for a reflection of the fire—and with hope.

Somebody suggested a walk to the shore of the lake, maybe to see the hippos feed there at night. All agreed loudly, and soon, one behind the other, between the clumps of giant papyrus reeds, they stumbled through the darkness. They had to cross over hippopotamus tracks filled with water like a row of bathtubs set in the mud. Their muted screams warded off the dangers of the bush.

They emerged on the shore and slowly separated. Some sat down. Some remained standing on the water's edge, silent. All thoughts hesitantly escaped them. Under the enormous canopy of the southern sky powdered with stars, the lake was black and roaring with the mating music of millions of creatures. A thin purple line, the horizon of the Rift Valley was faintly visible, a memory of the day. They were motionless, each one alone.

Then, without warning, it happened: African night.

LIAR

DURING THE BIG WAR a large part of Polish Gdansk was bombed out of existence. The sandy sea shore west of town remained untouched, it being strategically unimportant to Allied air forces. There, on the beach, I found a structure strategically significant to me. After a week's stay on the hay in the attic of a barn in nearby Kashuba village, the vision of this hotel promised great civilization. I could almost smell the freshly brewed coffee and the moist chocolate cake. The coffee would not be instant, and the cake would be topped with a heap of sweet cream, since Poles had not yet learned how to cheat using the chemistry of artificial sweeteners and creamers. Because of this illusion, I remained undeterred by the facade of the building which showed the effect of many decades of salty winds and Baltic winter storms. One was just in the making when I walked in.

I entered a silent refuge that was in marked contrast to the barn in Kashuba village. The room was immense, like a ballroom. A skylight flooded it with light of unexpected intensity for the shore of a sea notorious for its winter grimness. Another flood of creamy soft textured light came from the row of glass doors facing the beach. On the walls, the frescoes of seductively bent women in long robes in art nouveau design held bouquets of blossoms unknown to botanists. Mosaics of lions yawning in aggressive poses and halved pillars with pseudo-Corinthian heads supporting nothing—it all suggested the 1920s.

I selected one of about fifty tables with rose-colored marble tops and curved black metal legs. There were only two occupied tables in the whole room. At one, close to the entrance, two Catholic priests were engrossed in what seemed like an unfriendly discussion. All in black, their white faces leaned toward one another over their glasses of white wine; their lips moved in hushed tones, never gesticulating. Between me and the wall of glass doors, there was a table occupied by two women. Their silhouettes were dark and sharply outlined against the light. Both wore sprawling hats, and both smoked cigarettes in long holders. Swirls of smoke softened their sharp features periodically, kindly concealing the creased cheeks where layers of makeup had failed. I did not attempt to guess their ages.

Just after I ordered my dinner from a waiter (whose face would please Federico Fellini), the music started. From somewhere within the building the clear song of a violin unexpectedly penetrated the silence, then a wind instrument accentuated by what might have been cello-colored tones. It was the non-rhythm of contemporary abstract music to which the women sipped their wine, holding their glasses at the stems and their cigarettes with straightened fingers, their movements deliberately exaggerated. Outside, the mist was blown onto the beach from the increasingly restless sea. The dissonant violin slowed down as if batons of cigarette holders directed the invisible orchestra to moderato. I thought the scene was unreal and fantastic, and I was so taken by it that it took time before I noticed a new guest at the table next to me.

The waiter was talking in German, of which the young man apparently had no comprehension, so the guest raised his midwestern American voice and separated his words in hope that the waiter would understand that he was hungry and badly needed a beer. The old waiter still did not understand. Excusing myself, I offered help. I suspected that the young man had been having similar problems with communication for some time because he accepted my offer for him to join me at my table without hesitation.

His light northern hair was cropped quite conservatively for the fashion of the times. His face was attractive in its slight asymmetry—my mother would say he looked like a movie actor, that he had the bones. I thought his own mother would not have known any man more handsome. A pair of wrinkles at the corners of his mouth and three shallow creases on his forehead gave his age away as over thirty. He wore the uniform which by now has spanned over two generations: well-worn jeans, a T-shirt (with "Twins" on it), and a pair of moccasins.

"Kent Dreher," he said. "I'd need a magnifying glass for these." He pointed at the two triangular open face sandwiches on his plate, and while I introduced myself as briefly as he did, one sandwich was already gone.

"I don't want to sound like a redneck, but one big round pizza with anchovies and a blob of cheese on it—Shakey's—that would save me, my friend. And pepperoni on it too." Contemplatively, he shook his head looking at his now empty plate. "*Muj kamarade!*" he added, sort of for himself. This expression was not Polish. It said "my friend" in Czech, and because that is my native tongue it surprised me, almost as much as the abstract music over the silhouettes from a half century ago. The Czech expression from an American in Poland promised an interesting conversation. But since I call America my home now and consider myself an American, our communication continued only haltingly at first. The reason for that I have to explain.

I have observed that when two American strangers meet on their home turf—in the elevator of the IDS tower in Minneapolis, for instance—they remark first on the weather forecast, switch to problems in their work, and by the thirtieth floor confess to the pain of having a kid who wants to quit college or to a spouse who likes in-laws too much. When two Americans meet in faraway Amsterdam it will take some time spent in immediate proximity before they acknowledge one another but eventually they will progress to the weather and to where they come from. When two Americans meet anywhere in a Third World country a strange thing happens to their conversation. On a train from Madras to Madurai, for instance, it takes all the way to Kunda Hills before one says "hi" to the other. And in a microbus from Lagos to Enugu one would offer his or her name no sooner than the bridge over the Niger River. (It gets a little better in a Fourth World country, mostly because one is constantly sick and deprived of everything. Meeting a fellow First-Worlder offers an opportunity to milk that person for some survival information or to at least bum a cigarette.)

Since Poland was much like the Third World in the times of communist rule, we did not do so well conversing. But this had improved after two rounds of cognac, the price of which equaled a tenth of our waiter's monthly wages. So I suggested to Kent that we move to "my" village, which is not too far and has a drinking establishment. When I explained to my new acquaintance that it was not a classy restaurant or pub but just a simple native place, he agreed. I got the impression that he was on a tight budget. He planned to leave for Warsaw and then fly home in two days. I was still determined, though, to find out why he used the Czech expression *"muj kamarade."*

☙

We got lucky and waved down a truck right in front of the hotel. They do not hitchhike much in Poland. I felt elated by this fast lift, but I noticed that my companion continued to be in a subdued mood. It seemed that he was bothered by something in his past—our present circumstances were clearly favorable.

The truck dropped us at the edge of the village. Kent carefully separated five cigarettes from his pack of Polish brand for the driver, and we started marching through the village. It was a windy, cold night and so dark we had to concentrate, placing our steps cautiously. We walked in silence interrupted by an occasional profanity when one of us slipped or stumbled on the frozen mud. All the houses seemed uninhabited except one on the left side. Light and music poured from one window facing the road. We both got the same idea and turned stealthily to the house to approach the window.

The room was painted a glossy green, with a picture of a saint on one wall and on the opposite a poster of the dockyard with an inscription and exclamation marks printed over it in red. A broad bed filled one corner and a table with a plastic tablecloth stood by one wall. On a small stand in the corner there was an ancient model radio with a bottle on it, and in the bottle a paper flower. To the music of the radio an older man and woman danced. Their faces had many wrinkles and ancient eyes from which emanated happiness. It was the kind of unconditional happiness that one can see in children who do not yet know. (Also, I cannot forget the faces because of their background— the humiliating poverty of it. Not that kind of primitive simplicity one finds in the jungle's basic abode but the poverty that features the proud possession of a plastic radio decorated with a paper flower.) The couple danced slowly and talked, and their smiles did not leave them.

Stumbling away, we heard the music fading slowly, but the dancers' faces never faded in my mind.

"Did you see those people?" Kent said after a while. "They were actually happy there." Kent's observation made me feel very good and I looked forward to talking with him even more.

The drinking place appeared in front of us. It was good he noticed—because I was still thinking about the old couple. We found a rickety table in the corner and ordered the Polish classic—vodka. There were no frescoes of roaring lions or sighing ladies in flowing robes on the walls here. Instead of Fellini's waiter, a strong woman in an apron put a bottle of clear fluid in front of us with a thump. It is impossible to guess the age of somebody who does not have any teeth, and her lack of them might have been why she did not smile or talk. She brought Wodka Zwykla, the cheapest brand, made from fermented potatoes, diluted by water. It tastes like that. It comes in green tinted bottles, and the labels look like pieces of newspaper and are usually half-peeled off. The bottles are corked—not by such an exotic material as the bark of the cork oak, but by some kind of matter resembling gray sealing-wax, which crumbles when broken off and the crumbs fall into the bottle and have to be spat out when drinking the contents. But this alcohol warmed us pleasantly and loosened our tongues.

Between shots of vodka drunk "*do dna*" (bottoms up) as local custom demands, I listened to the history of the midwesterner Kent Dreher. He had a Boy Scout and high school football background, then muddled through indecisions in college complicated by involvement in various causes, all expected from a liberal young Minnesotan. His story was inconsequential—until Kent recalled the time last year when he met a Czech refugee at a party on the University's West Bank.

"He was a quiet fellow—drank a lot, though," Kent said. "I asked him about agriculture, collective farming, self-help, and that sort of thing." Kent could still concentrate, since we had slowed down on our drinking. "He had a deadly accent."

A few weeks passed before Kent met this man again. They ran into each other in a bar across from a concert hall in downtown Minneapolis. After drinking a few Summit Ales, the Czech narrated an immigrant story of having a girlfriend back in the old country and how he loved her more and more as their time of separation increased and how he would give anything, everything, for them to get together again and get married.

"I could see this guy was serious—he had this sincere face, even as he got more and more drunk." Kent downed another vodka without paying it any attention. "He seemed sort of perpetually depressed. As I am now," Kent added. In the bar across from the concert hall, Kent learned that the Czech was looking for somebody to go to Prague to marry his girlfriend, Katerina.

"'That is the only way she can get a passport and a fucking exit permit from those Bolsheviks to come over to America,' the Czech explained. 'And once here she can apply for political asylum. No risk at all if absolutely no one in Prague knows the truth about the marriage—absolutely nobody.'"

They had talked until closing time because Kent had become seriously interested. If he went, his round trip would be paid for by his new acquaintance and he would be able to visit the collective farm, too. Kent promised to sit on it for a few days, to think it over when he was sober. In a couple of months the arrangements for the marriage in Prague had been made. Kent made reservations on a Northwest flight to Frankfurt and a train from there to Prague. He was to spend a few days after the wedding looking around and then fly home. Katerina would remain in Prague and work on her emigration papers.

∾

On the first of May, Kent arrived at Main Station in Prague. A cowboy hat identified him for the waiting Katerina and two of her friends, both proficient in English. One was the owner of a car and the other of an apartment with a spare room for Kent. He thought the idea of a cowboy hat was pretty corny—but it worked perfectly. Katerina was quietly nervous, uneasy in her English, and kept behind when they walked to the car. Her friends were exuberant, asking questions about Kent's trip and insisting on carrying his suitcase. They were obviously impressed by his wide-brimmed Stetson. They drove past processions of mandatory participants in a May Day parade who carried red banners with the hammer and sickle design. Kent was surprised by the sudden feeling of fear around his stomach and wondered, just briefly, if his adventure indeed promised a safe outcome—a safe ending meaning departure from Prague and the crossing over the border at the scheduled time. His new friends seemed not to pay any attention to the street. They were absorbed in their new American.

The strong woman in the apron brought us a plate with cylindrical pieces of smoked meat. "*Wengorz wendzony*," she said, waiting for us to make a gesture of appreciation. Which I did and translated to Kent that he was about to taste the best food available on these shores: home smoked eel.

"Snake," Kent said, but devoured it with relish, washing it down with vodka as a native would do. Then he elaborated on the story about his marriage in the medieval city hall of ancient Prague, in front of the stern clerk with a translator at his side who watched closely, with open mouth, Kent's fleeting wedding kiss. From the speakers hung in round corners of the Gothic hall they played the obligatory Mendelssohn wedding march while all of Katerina's friends shook Kent's hand, and looking into his eyes, one by one, assured him how happy they were that it was he who married her. They wished them a hundred years of happiness together.

"Hundred years, my ass!" Kent said. "But I liked them from the beginning. I really did." He was leaning over the table towards me. "You see, I was damn sure they all meant it." He paused and ordered two glasses of water from the strong woman, in English. She just continued walking away.

"That's when my trouble started, right there," he said. "I never expected this kind of problem. I expected the communists getting at me, maybe. Police, secret police." He pounded the table once with his hand rocking my shot glass. "But never this kind of trouble."

I wasn't clear yet as to the nature of his problem and why he was raising his voice. He continued after a while.

"After the ceremony, about five or six of us went to a nearby restaurant and drank there. A lot," he said, in a lower voice now. "Katerina's friend Ivan, he's a goldsmith with long hair. He comes to me and tells me how she is lucky to have a man, a husband, like me and about how I would make her life happy and that he, Ivan, would remain my friend forever. He put his arms around me." I looked into Kent's eyes, but he lowered them into his vodka.

"And I lied to him. Right there I said I would take care of her always," Kent said. "I felt like shit, but I lied without blinking an eye, man." He continued. "Then this real mellow guy, Bohous, came up to me. I had heard that he used to go with Katerina some years before. We drank a few of those slivovitzes together. He told me how he, and everybody else, liked me and how happy they were I was taking her to the U.S. and how he would do anything for me because he felt how honest a guy I was. Honest guy! Then he apologized for talking like that, but he had had to say it. He would wait for me to come back with Katerina to Prague soon and we would all go fishing and camping somewhere in South Bohemia."

Kent was talking as if to himself, quietly. His eyes looked red, but it might have been caused by just too much vodka.

"And I told him, yes, I would take care of her, my new wife. My wife, man! And when we came back here again we would try fly-fishing," Kent told him. "And when my voice trembled, you know, his started to tremble, too. He put his hand on my shoulder and told me it was okay, that guys like me even cry over good things. That it was all right to do that." Kent did not look happy at all. He continued, "You see, I lied to all of them. I just lied. They could not know that in truth I was a fake. It would be too dangerous."

It was getting late and most of the Kashuba fishermen had stumbled out of the drinking place. There were just two left, who, I think, were not able to get up.

Kent told me how his new friends divided their time into shifts and took him every day around the historic city, to a restaurant of famous artists, and to another where they had been brewing their own beer since the fifteenth century, and to another where *The Good Soldier Swejk* had been written. They took him to a church with a relic of a dried arm, hanging there for hundreds of years. In another baroque cathedral, so golden and mysterious that he did not ever want to leave, he almost told them the whole truth. "There I forgot that I was just a goddamn liar and cheat," Kent said.

Katerina sometimes went with them on these expeditions through the magic city. Every day Kent met her. That is all he said. I wanted to ask more about her. Much more. But I felt that I should not.

We emptied the last shot of vodka, not toasting anything.

"Goddamn liar. You don't know how it feels," Kent continued. "They were real friends. And still I have not told you the whole story, *muj kamarade*."

⚭

It was time, I thought, to save Kent from more of this hardship. So I got up, stretched, walked to the window, and looked into the darkness. There was a hint of dawn behind the dunes piled up along the shore, their contours outlined as if by a pink pencil. When I returned Kent was staring at the empty bottle, trying to peel off the label.

"Do you know, Kent, about the Kashuba people in this village?" I asked. "Strange folks, you know. They speak a kind of German dialect. They are supposed to have been settled here for centuries, right next to those Slavic Poles. Fishermen, always." I wanted to lighten up the situation. And for Kent to straighten up a little.

"They were supposed to have migrated to this shore in very ancient times. Maybe in the old Neanderthal times," I tried to joke, feebly.

"Yah, from *Australopithecus* times. Right?" Kent surprised me, responding with an imitation drunken mumbling. He definitely looked brighter.

"Hey, Kent, from *Australopithecus afarensis*. How's that?" I showed off. "Which reminds me," I continued, "of when I was in Nairobi, years ago, in the Kenya Anthropology Museum. There it was, the famous skull of 'Lucy.' *Australopithecus afarensis* . . . I presume? And you know," I said, "what I did? I kissed that Lucy. Right on the upper jaw. I kissed her!" With the idiotic expression of a winner, I waited for Kent to respond.

Kent did not laugh. He leaned back in his chair and looked at me with a composed expression. I was surprised by the abrupt end to our fooling around.

"I kissed, too, my friend," Kent calmly said after a while. "I kissed her first at the wedding ceremony. Then the next day I kissed her. This is what I did not want to tell you." And he added, while looking at his feet, "And again, and again, and more."

∾

It was time to leave. We got up, paid, and walked into the deserted street. "Let's have a coffee at my place," I suggested. My place was the attic of a barn, where a Kashuba lady let me stay for a week for five yards of "*plusz*," imitation fur. It smelled nicely of hay there, and it was warm. We climbed up the sturdy ladder. I rolled a bunch of hay into my towel for Kent's pillow, which he took with his first smile of the evening. I started up my gasoline camping stove on the straw covered floor and made us up a cup of sweet instant coffee—without setting the hay, the bar, and Kashuba village ablaze.

A shy light penetrated into our cave between the planks of the attic. The clean and hopeful time of early morning was beginning.

Kent Dreher told me "Goodnight" and covered himself with hay.

"Thank you, Kent," I said. "I'll have one more smoke."

I watched him struggling for sleep, turning fitfully from side to side. Then with a hand over his eyes he became motionless, his expression finally peaceful.

Liar he was, perhaps, but he was the best man I have met in a long, long time.

SHADOWS OF
THE BAOBAB TREE

The baobab stands upside down—
Old Dinka people say.
The branches underground
Not roots
Are searching Earth for wisdom.
But all in vain.
"The tree where man was born?"
One does not wonder.

Lenny coursiere is my name. I am thirty-four years old but I look older. I was born and raised in Beroun, Minnesota, my father's hometown. He never traveled, never wandered out of Beroun despite his name, Coursiere, and therefore his conviction that he is a descendant of restless Quebec voyageurs. There is some Chippewa Indian blood in his ancestry of which he seems to be proud. About my mother's relatives little is known to me, except that they came from Scandinavia and never volunteered to discuss the old country or their family. They did not talk much about anything, that side of my family.

I am barely five foot four and, some say, of ascetic appearance. In fact it is an asthenic constitution, which is not a result of ascetic habits. I might have inherited this stature from my paternal grandmother who is remembered as the thinnest person in Beroun. When she did not wake up from her sleep at ninety-six years of age, it was believed to be the outcome of dessication. The doctor, who examined her remains, found all her internal organs shriveled and completely dried up. So it was transmitted to me. I believe it is possible that my withered condition could partially come from excessive drinking—alcohol is known to be a drying agent. Sometimes I ask myself if my feeble body is related to psychological fragility and to what my acquaintances consider an exaggerated fear of violence.

Presently, I find myself employed as a consular officer in the American embassy in Al-Barahud. I spent three years in France in a similar position but because of my personal problems I was transferred here to the desert. My fluency in French and partial knowledge of Arabic was the official reason and the one I wrote about to my dad. The unofficial reason, known to all my colleagues, was the unavailability of liquor in this country of baobab trees and sand. Arrack distillate is smuggled in here but one needs an accomplice to obtain it, and to accomplices one has to admit the need for a drink. And they hated it in the embassy in Paris so much that I have never admitted to this need, never admitted to being an alcoholic. So good did I become in covering my tracks that even my best pal Lance never knew for sure. The more I drank the more refined my deceptions became and, in turn, the more strain I had to withstand. Something had to be done. I realized that too.

I remember clearly my arrival in Al-Barahud. The plane descended low over the sea, so low that I could recognize the patches on a sail of a fishing dhow, then the white lace of the surf, one second of a brown sandy beach, a sage covered dune, and then a glimpse of a baobab tree—the hallmark of this continent, "the tree where man was born." The airplane dropped even lower, over the head of a shepherd in white robe standing motionless near the runway, seemingly undisturbed by the fast flying shadow of the jet plane. His small herd of goats panicked just for a moment, though.

I forced myself not to finish the gin and tonic as a show of my will, of my decision to halt for good the difficult ailment of drinking. I held the unfinished drink on the floor between my shoes when we touched down. The roar of engines increased, then died.

∽

One sunny morning (there are no other than sunny mornings here), about a month after arrival, I went to the airport again to pick up our new decoding man coming in from Paris. The plane was late but in the airport terminal the air conditioning worked so I was not distracted by the usual stream of salty sweat into my eyes and I could enjoy watching the waiting crowd. I felt good. I could actually sense my fitness—the muscles, the lungs. I savored the new found health in the whole geography of my body. It had been four weeks since my last drink, the half-finished gin and tonic on the plane approaching the airport from the sea over the baobab tree. True, I became a social solitary even more than I had been in Paris, but this sober condition brought me strength I have not known for years.

Next to me, the two nomadic Tuaregs in dark blue robes and loosely wound turbans did not change their royal expression and posture when the 747 touched down and the waiting crowd stirred. I used my diplomatic passport to persuade the submachine gun bearers by the entrance to let me go onto the tarmac together with the service personnel.

The staircase was pulled to the plane and soon the stewardess appeared with the usual smile. Passengers started to emerge and descend the stairs, some waving at the building. Some, startled by the light and heat clutched the railing, wavered as in haze. Most wore business suits. A few had white robes and some had *ghutra* on their heads. There was one old woman in traditional dress. Her *abaaya*, veiling her face and eyes, made her steps uncertain. I watched for the decoding man, whom I remembered from Paris.

A young woman emerged from the plane in a long-sleeved blouse and a long skirt, with a gray scarf covering her hair. She did not look around as all the other passengers did, her attention was only on the stairs. A middle-aged man in a dark suit and smaller than she followed her. On the first step of the staircase he hit her face from behind. Then he hit her again with a more powerful blow. She stumbled, not raising her hands in defense, and continued slowly down the stairs, as if she were shaken merely by a blast of wind she had anticipated. The stewardess attending the bottom of the stairs saw the incident, moved forward, but retreated a step back and averted her eyes.

Violence always affects me strangely. I could not breathe or move and felt the swell of burning heat in my face.

The young woman descended to the tarmac followed by the

small man. She did not turn when he kicked her leg from behind. She started limping then, passing so close to me that I could see her face clearly. She was pale, beautiful, with very big eyes from which tears streamed. She expressed something I could not understand in that moment of stress. An armed guard started to approach the man then, but stopped and started to adjust his gun, looking to the ground. The girl limped into the building followed by the small man.

I did not notice the decoding man till he took my hand and shook it several times. Only in the car did I manage to compose myself. I told him what I saw, but not about her face.

∽

This is what came to my desk from the U.S. in the case of Amal Farahat: simple instructions to gather the relevant information about her. Relevant? In the text of instructions I could read between the lines an order "not to make waves." This waves business is the golden rule in almost all matters in our embassy and the torturous lingo by which it is conveyed is well understood by employees at all levels. Farahat's story had the potential of trouble. The first problem was that she was an American citizen, born in New Jersey. But her parents, immigrants from Al-Barahud, were not. The second problem, as it appeared between the lines, was the wealth of her father—and because of that, his connections to powerful people.

The case became a "case" when the parents of one of Amal's school mates alerted the State Department that Amal Farahat was leaving the country against her will and under circumstances they described as "suspicious." These circumstances were being investigated by a special agency at the request of the State Department.

I broke the seal of another report in the file and learned that Amal was an above average student in her senior year at Roosevelt High and was well-liked by her peers. After each expedition to a school dance and twice to discos, the next day she would come to school with signs of abuse. A black eye once, a swollen cheek and lips another time, and bruises on places she could reveal only to her female friends. She never complained, but it became obvious from her remarks that her father forbade her to date, to associate with anybody he did not approve of, or to go out of the house after school. The conclusion to this report hypothesized that the father's cultural and religious traditions and ways required severe punishment of all in his family who disobeyed him. For reasons not obvious to me, this report had not been acted upon since it was marked "inactive"—until our embassy requested it. I became nervous and agitated while reading the file.

There were only two other documents included. One stated that two complaints had been filed with the New Jersey State Police Department against Mr. Farahat on suspicion of domestic violence and the abuse of his daughter Amal. Nobody had investigated these reports nor followed up on them.

Chronologically, the last document was a copy of an anonymous letter of two laser-printed pages. In business language it stated that Mr. Farahat had sold all his assets and holdings, including the house in New Jersey and two parcels of industrial real estate, closed his business, and traded in his investments. He transferred large sums of money to the national bank in his country of origin. The last paragraph in the document questioned the reasons for these transactions and under an asterisk quoted the opinion of an unnamed associate of Farahat's. It was his conviction that Mr. Farahat was going to leave the U.S. permanently because he believed that he was being prevented from controlling his daughter by means his cultural traditions suggest and he prefers.

I was struggling with this file trying to figure out how I could even start to gather more information and I was even questioning the sense of it all. My vacation was imminent in a few weeks and that bright prospect occupied my mind with more urgency than all this Farahat business. With every passing day and week of the drudgery here, the lake country of Minnesota looked more and more like an unreal mirage to me, a *fata morgana* from heaven. The sand there would not be oven-hot and blowing into my eyes but it would be wet on the beach of a cool crystal lake.

∽

On May 8th, Rodrigo Camargo called me into his office on the second floor. I remember the day well, since it was Tuesday, and each

Tuesday embassy employees were allowed the use of the university swimming pool with other foreigners suffering in Al-Barahud. Ladies had the morning, men the afternoon. It was always the brightest day of my week, not only because of the water but because of the interesting people who gathered around the pool.

Karol "Killer" Kowalski (KKK), the Polish engineer, is always there with his pal Jerzy "Lily of the Valley" Jastrowski. They translate Polish jokes into English, which nobody gets but they all laugh anyway. (I promised to memorize the tongue twister, *chrzonst brzmi v trzstine*.) Jerzy smokes continuously, even in the water. The Swedish contingent thinks he is an idiot. I also like Omar El Deeb, the dentist from Cairo, built like Golem, with the enormous fists of an ex-boxing champion of Egypt. Welter-weight. I know his heart must be bigger than his fists—he never forgets a six-pack of "Star" Nigerian pilsner in his little brown backpack and distributes the treasure to the less fortunate ones around the pool. He has repeatedly proclaimed his dislike of the natives and their customs (like stoning women to death). For this reason he has founded and coaches the Al-Barahud Boxing Club with the sole purpose of "beating up the natives legally. To pulp." Then there is Niels Clauson of Uppsala, Sweden. He never misses a swim day either. He explains to everyone who likes Omar's beer and views, that one should not judge the local culture by our Western standards. An asshole, but a great swimmer—one has to grant him that. He can swim the length of the pool in seven butterfly strokes. And Pietro, the architect, plays guitar like a pro and after a couple of beers can mimic a mezzosoprano castrato so effectively he can bring his audience to tears. He is from near Napoli, of course.

As I said, Rodrigo Camargo called me to his office. Behind his cluttered desk that sat under Old Glory and a sincere photo of the president, he was sweating. Which was not unusual since he always sweats, air conditioning or not.

"Lenny, this is shit. I hate these things happening," he mumbled without greeting me. Since he did not look at me and shuffled his papers urgently on his desk, I suspected trouble. "You must be careful, Lenny, you know these bastards by now."

He sighed.

"What's the problem, Rodrigo?" I sat down, trying to look relaxed. "But first tell me, are you going after lunch? Swimming?"

"Forget it." He looked at me, then at the ceiling. "I shouldn't do this to you, but there is nobody else in this circus I can send today."

He told me that there was a corpse in the morgue, in the hospital by that big baobab tree. He said that the corpse had American citizenship, so the police called him and the police chief, the only one who speaks some English, said that there had been a car accident— a hit and run. They found the victim on a garbage pile by the market two days ago. But all that was obviously bullshit, Rodrigo told me. He made it clear that I just had to go to the morgue and have a look, copy down what was in the autopsy, get the police statement, put it together somehow, and write it up as a presentable report.

"And make it simple, *compadre*, simple and no opinions, no bull about what you think and so on. *Por favor?*" Rodrigo looked worried and obviously unhappy about all this, tapping his index finger on the head of the miniature Statue of Liberty on his desk. "These things always create headaches. And worse," he said, and banged the head of Liberty, avoiding her raised hand with the torch. "You know what I mean?"

I did not, really, and I was pretty unhappy about the missed chance to go swimming. Rodrigo gave me his "*Jesu Maria, tengo problema enorme*" look, so I told him not to worry, that I'd muddle through somehow and write it up right away. Tomorrow, maybe. No problem for me. I lied because he looked so down about it and because I liked him, his hopeless accent, the pencil mustache of a crook, and his confession that he used to be a drunk on Tequila back State-side, which made him a soul mate of sorts.

ॐ

The biggest baobab in town stood in front of the hospital. For this season it had shed all its leaves. One wouldn't know if it were dead or just pretending. It denied any shade to the building, its shadow just drawing sharp convoluted lines on the whitewashed stucco, like a giant crawling insect.

In the hospital, the orderly, an elderly fellow with the dark leather face of a Bedouin, showed me the door. He would not enter with me, avoided my eyes and my question about who did the post mortem, and silently disappeared.

By the wall of the empty room stood an elevated metal table on rollers and on it lay the body covered with a green sheet. Bright light flooded the room from a large horizontal window, through which I noticed one black arm of the baobab, branching into curved fingers which touched the window. The whiteness of the walls hurt my eyes. The immense room was empty of sound. I turned around, opened the door, and propped it ajar to diminish the privacy of my situation. I coughed to disturb the silence.

"I will uncover the face fast and cover it again. I think I can do it. I will make 'an attempt at identification,' and then get out. I'll go upstairs after that to find out who did the post mortem. This is tough business. I don't feel so good."

I shuffled closer to the table. The left hand of the body lay exposed. It was clearly the hand of a female. The slender fingers were gray and her short fingernails were bluish with specks of red nail polish. Around her wrist was a ring of bruised skin. It was almost black, the bruised skin, like a rope burn. I looked back at the door, surprised by a sudden feeling of danger. But I was alone.

I approached the body and lifted the green sheet covering her face—the face I have remembered every day since the airport incident.

∾

The dark claws of the baobabs seem to curve down at me, the softness of shade is nowhere to be found, the sun's rays burn me, the light makes the shadows black. I am lost in them. I drink Arrack liquor every evening now. It softens the razors of the silhouettes and sometimes chases away the moving shadows.

Only her face with those eyes does not leave me. It remains flooded with blinding light.

That is all I have to say—that I am not the same, not the same Lenny as before.

About the Author

Jaroslav (Jarda) Cervenka was born and raised in Prague, where he studied medicine and, later, human genetics. During the Soviet invasion in 1968, he emigrated to Minnesota, where he teaches at the University of Minnesota. *Mal d'Afrique* is his first book of stories.

Mr. Cervenka has visited the Cholos of Columbia, Inuit in Canada, Tamils in South India and Sri Lanka, Polynesians in most Pacific Island states, mountain tribes of the Golden Triangle in Thailand, many African tribes, Slavs of Europe, and others. His interest in diving and mountaineering have taken him to the islands of the Pacific and Indian Oceans, the South China Sea and the Caribbean, to Kilimanjaro, Fuji, Mt. Fengari, and Aconcagua. These extensive travel experiences—combined with Mr. Cervenka's memories and experiences from his native Bohemia have become a rich well of complex human fates reflected in this collection of stories.